SCARY STORIES

FOR SLEEP-OVERS #10

Mark Kehl

ROXBURY PARK

LOWELL HOUSE JUVENILE

LOS ANGELES

NTC/Contemporary Publishing Group

Published by Lowell House
A division of NTC/Contemporary Publishing Group, Inc.
4255 West Touhy Avenue, Lincolnwood (Chicago), Illinois 60646-1975 U.S.A.

ISBN: 0-7373-0114-7
Library of Congress Catalog Card Number: 99-71715

Lowell House books can be purchased at special discounts when ordered
in bulk for premiums and special sales. Contact Department CS at the
following address:
NTC/Contemporary Publishing Group
4255 West Touhy Avenue
Lincolnwood, IL 60646-1975
1-800-323-4900

Roxbury Park is a division of NTC/Contemporary Publishing Group, Inc.

Managing Director and Publisher: Jack Artenstein
Editor in Chief, Roxbury Park: Michael Artenstein
Director of Publishing Services: Rena Copperman
Editorial Assistant: Nicole Monastirsky
Interior Designer: Treesha Runnells Vaux

Printed and bound in the United States of America

10 9 8 7 6 5 4 3 2 1

Contents

The Crispy Hand

Rich and Tommy had heard the tale a million times—
every time they visited their grandmother. When they
were younger, it used to keep them up at night. But Tommy
was 12 now, Rich 14, and they were tired of hearing about
the Crispy Hand.

However, the story was a tradition and unavoidable. So
after an excellent dinner of ham and Grandma's secret-
recipe mashed potatoes, and after Rich and Tommy had
done the dishes, the boys gathered in the living room, where
their mother and grandmother were drinking tea.

"Tommy, would you throw another log on the fire,
please?" his grandmother asked. She gave him a sinister
smile. "You'll want all the light you can get after you hear
the story of . . . the Crispy Hand!"

Tommy restrained himself from rolling his eyes as he
moved to the wood bin. He fed the fire a split chunk of oak
and then sat on the hearth to enjoy the heat. Rich sat with
their mother on the sofa. Grandma was in her chair close to
the fire, an afghan wrapped around her legs. She held her
teacup and saucer in her lap, where they occasionally rattled
from her trembling.

"A long, long time ago," she began, "something bad
happened in this very town."

Rich mouthed the words along with her. Tommy had to

put his hand over his own mouth to keep from laughing. Their mom knew how tired they were of this story—they had complained about it all afternoon during the car ride— but she had told them to show respect for their grandmother and to listen. Their mom nudged Rich to make him stop, and Tommy focused on Grandma so he wouldn't be tempted to laugh by watching any further antics of his brother.

"Before I was born, when most of the land around town was still forest, the townspeople were very suspicious of outsiders. Back then, people didn't travel as much as they do today. You didn't just hop into your car and drive four hours to see your grandma. You saw more horses on the road than automobiles, and there were no airplanes. Our town was ten miles from the nearest railroad line. So not too many strangers passed through these parts, and when they did the townsfolk made good and sure to find out their business and keep an eye on them."

Tommy risked a glance at Rich, but he was behaving himself now, becoming engrossed in the story despite himself.

"One day, as dusk was thickening into night, the town constable got word that there was a stranger walking on the forest road toward town. A farmer heading into town had spotted the man, large and hairy like a bear, and word spread through the small town like wildfire. So the constable and his deputies rode out to meet this stranger. The constable rode a fine chestnut mare. The two deputies followed with the police wagon hitched to a team.

"They had no problem finding the stranger. He was walking along the side of the road, just as they'd been told. However, he wasn't the bear of a man they expected. He was tall, yes, but his big coat hung on him as if he were made of broomsticks. His dark hair hadn't been cut in a long time. Between it and his thick facial hair, he *did* look a lot like an animal. But not a fierce one—just a tired and hungry one.

"The constable pulled up in front of the man. Letting the stranger get a good look at his rifle, he asked his name and his business. The stranger stared wearily and then shook his head. The constable raised his voice and asked again. The stranger held out his empty hands and in a deep, rough voice said something in a language the constable did not understand. Neither did his deputies.

"So the constable ordered his deputies to lock up the man in the police wagon. The stranger didn't understand as they stepped warily toward him, but when they tried to grab him he struggled fiercely. However, he was no match for the two strong deputies, and they locked him in the police wagon.

"'We'll let him spend a night in jail,' the constable said. 'Tomorrow we'll let him loose a few miles up the Barnesville Road. That'll let him know his kind ain't welcome here.'

"The deputies knew this routine well—that's what they did with any stranger who came to their town without a darn good reason. So they drove the wagon back to the jail, which in those days was an old timber building that had been around longer than any other building in town. They used to say that the rebels locked up British loyalists there during the Revolutionary War. It was a squat building made of rough-hewn logs that had turned black with age, and it had crude iron bars over the windows. It was old, but it did the job. Kind of like me."

Tommy and the others smiled at the familiar joke.

"The deputies did as they were told. They took the

stranger to the jail and locked him up, the only prisoner there."

Grandma paused to sip her tea. *What a horrible place to stop*, Tommy thought, knowing what came next and wishing she would get it over with. Grandma took a second sip of tea and then resumed the story.

"No one knows how the fire started, but in a wooden building of that age it came as no surprise. It was cold that time of year, and the heat came from an old coal stove. Maybe a stray ember landed on the roof, or maybe a bird had made a nest in the chimney, or maybe one of the deputies had been careless with the stove door, allowing a spark to jump out. The cells were full of old straw for prisoners to sleep on. That straw made good tinder, and before you knew it, that old wooden jail was one big bonfire.

"As soon as someone spotted the fire, they rang the church bell. In those days, everybody in town dropped whatever they were doing and came to fight a fire. There were no hydrants or fire trucks, so they had to use buckets. They formed long lines stretching from well pumps to the fire. Then they passed the full buckets along the line and the empty ones back. Not the best way to fight a fire, but the best they could do.

"They tried to save the jail, but it just burned too fast. Even with four lines feeding buckets of water, it was like spitting on a campfire. But they tried, and all the while the townspeople could hear the strange foreign shouts of the stranger in his cell.

"Finally, the heat became too fierce, and they couldn't get close enough to throw their buckets of water on the flames. It was a lost cause, and they all knew it. Somberly, they watched the jail burn. From one window, a hand reached through the bars, grasping at life and freedom. Its fingers clutched and strained as the horrified people watched. Strange foreign screams rose from the heart of the blaze."

Tommy decided he was warm enough and moved away from the fireplace to sit on the sofa with Rich and his mom.

"The next morning the jail was nothing more than smoking ash and cinders," Grandma continued. "The constable and his deputies sifted through it but found no sign of their prisoner, not even the hand that had tried so hard to reach freedom. With nothing to bury, they shrugged and started to clean up the mess. They had a new jail to think about. They forgot all about the stranger whom they had, in a manner of speaking, murdered.

"That night, as one of the deputies lay in his bed, he heard something. He lived by himself and had no pets, but he could tell something was in the house with him. He heard a soft scuffling across the bare wood floor. *Mice,* he thought. Tomorrow, he told himself, he would get some traps. But tomorrow would never come for him, for a few moments later something locked around his throat. The thing seemed thin and brittle, but its grip was superhumanly strong. The deputy could not breathe. He tried to pry the thing free, but it clung too tightly.

"The constable found his body the next day when the deputy didn't show up for work. He was in bed, with the sheets and blankets all thrown about. His bloodshot eyes bulged from his face, and his bloated tongue protruded from his mouth. The oddest thing was what showed on his bruised neck: a set of sooty marks that looked as if they'd been made by the fingers of one hand."

Tommy found himself rubbing his neck, imagining the feel of charred fingers digging into the soft flesh.

"Well," Grandma continued, "the constable knew what people would think if they found out about the soot marks, so he kept that quiet. He was not a superstitious man and he knew there had to be some other explanation. Maybe the dead stranger had friends in the area who were trying to get revenge for his death. This seemed more plausible than the man's charred hand running around killing people. So he got his other deputy and some of the townsmen, and they rode around looking for strangers. But they found no one.

"That night, the second deputy, mourning the death of his friend, walked aimlessly around town, reeling from the shock. He was walking home after midnight when his scream woke half the town. Lanterns flared to life as people rushed to their windows to see what was going on. They saw the deputy lying facedown in the street. Those who got to him first, including the town doctor in his nightshirt, rolled him over. His dead eyes were wide with fright, and his throat was streaked with soot.

"The next day, stories of the Crispy Hand were all over town. It crept the streets at night, they said, and would not rest until its murderers had all felt its sooty grip. The constable redoubled his efforts to find a real, human culprit, but again he failed. By that evening, he was starting to have his doubts. Superstitious or not, all this talk about the Crispy Hand had him rattled. He was the only one left of the three who had locked up the stranger, and the sun was going down. He was scared.

"So when his wife said that she was ready for bed, he told her to go up without him. Then he made himself a full pot of strong black coffee. He made himself comfortable at the table and covered his lantern. In the darkness, he drank coffee to stay awake, keeping one hand on his gun.

"After midnight, he was starting to feel drowsy despite all that coffee. But then he heard a soft thump from the fireplace, and he was instantly wide awake, with all his senses focused to razor sharpness. *It came down the chimney,* he thought. He heard it scuttle through the ashes and scrabble across the hearth. Suddenly he threw back the cover of the lantern, and there it was."

Grandma made a sweeping gesture, and Tommy and the others flinched. Grandma had to grab at her teacup to keep it from toppling.

"The Crispy Hand was poised there on its fingers like some hideous five-legged spider. As soon as the constable rose from his chair, it skittered into the darkness behind the coal stove. Warily he approached, with the lantern dangling from one hand, and his revolver in the other. The hand scuttled away from the light, circling the stove. The constable gently holstered his revolver and picked up the tongs from the stove. The tongs clacked as he tested them, like giant iron tweezers. Then he set the lantern on the floor and began to circle the stove.

"The Crispy Hand retreated from him as before but seemed wary of the light from the lantern. As it seemed to hesitate, trapped between the constable and the lantern, the constable lunged. The tips of the tongs closed on the Crispy Hand. He lifted it from the floor and moved it closer to the lantern. Both fascinated and repulsed, he studied it in the light, a human hand, charred and blackened by fire, its skin flaked and mostly gone. But the most grotesque thing was the way it moved. Its fingers thrashed as if madly playing some invisible piano.

"Suddenly the constable could bear looking at the thing no longer. He threw open the door of the coal stove and thrust the hand in among the glowing red embers. Most horrible of all, *it would not burn*! Its fingers seemed to calm as they stirred the embers, and then it just sat there in that infernal heat as if waiting.

"The constable, growing angry with frustration, pulled out the hand and smashed it against the floor. He held it there with the tongs and stomped on it with his boots, but it did no good. The Crispy Hand seemed to be indestructible. He glared at the hand and cursed it. 'You'll not kill me, evil thing,' he vowed. And then he came up with a plan. If he could not destroy the hand, he could at least contain it so that it would not be able to creep up on him in a moment of vulnerability and strangle him, as it had his two deputies. So he put the hand into a stout wooden chest and slammed the lid closed before it could scramble out. Then he locked the chest and hid it away where no one would find it.

"And that," Grandma said, glorying in the conclusion of her tale, "is how the Crispy Hand came to be locked in the attic of this very house!"

∙∙∙∙∙∙∙∙∙∙∙

That night Rich and Tommy slept in twin beds in the guest room. At home they had their own rooms and liked it that way, but sleeping in the same room was fun once in a while. Tommy had his penlight, and they made shadows on the wall for a while. Then they spent a long time talking and laughing in the darkness. However, they stopped suddenly when they heard a skittering sound overhead.

"Ooh," Tommy said, "do you think it's the Crispy Hand?"

Rich snorted. "No, I think it's leaves blowing across the roof."

"Do you think it really happened? That someone died in the fire like Grandma says?"

"Maybe. She must have gotten the idea for the story somewhere. But you know what? I think I've figured out why she tells us that stupid story every time we come here."

"Why?" Tommy shone his penlight in Rich's face.

"Get that thing out of my eyes, or I'm not gonna tell you."

Tommy turned off the light. "So, why?"

"To keep us out of the attic. Think about it. As scared as we used to get about the Crispy Hand, we *never* would have dared going up there."

"Yeah," Tommy said, seeing his brother's point. "But why wouldn't she want us to go up there?"

"That's just it. That's the real question. What's up there she doesn't want us to see? As far as I know, nobody's been up there for years. Grandma certainly couldn't make it up there. If she went to all the trouble of making up that stupid story, whatever's up there has to be pretty good."

"I guess we could go up and look," Tommy said, throwing back his covers. "The trapdoor is in the closet in this room. And I've got my penlight."

He flashed it in Rich's eyes again.

"Turn that stupid thing off or I'm going to shove it down your throat."

Tommy turned it off, snickering.

"We can't go up now," Rich said. "Mom and Grandma would hear, and we don't want them to know we were in the attic, right?"

"Right," Tommy agreed.

"So we'll wait until tomorrow," Rich went on. "Mom and Grandma are planning to go to garage sales all morning. We can say that we want to stay here and build a fort in the woods or something. While they're gone, we can spend as much time looking around the attic as we like."

"That's a pretty good plan," Tommy said. "Sometimes, you can be pretty *bright.*"

He flashed the light in his brother's face again.

"That's it—you're dead!"

....

The boys' not wanting to go to garage sales came as no surprise to their mother, but she was still reluctant to leave them behind.

"What are you going to do here by yourselves?" she asked.

"Watch TV, eat, mess around in the woods," Rich said. "The same stuff we do at home."

"I don't want you two horsing around in your grandmother's house and breaking things."

"Naw, we won't," Tommy said. "We'll only break things outside."

Their mother sighed and looked at Grandma. "See what I have to put up with? Be glad you didn't have boys."

Grandma snorted. "No two boys could have been as big a handful as you and your sisters. It's okay if they stay here. They won't get into any mischief, right boys?"

The boys were reassuring as they hustled the two women out of the house. They watched through the window until the car was out of sight.

"Let's go!" Tommy shouted, racing for the closet that held the trapdoor to the attic. He got to the hallway before he realized his older brother wasn't following. "What are you waiting for?"

"I was just thinking about the way Grandma looked at us. She trusted us not to cause any trouble."

"We're not going to cause any trouble," Tommy said. "We're just going to go up into the attic and look around." Then a grin spread across his face. "Unless you're scared. Think the Crispy Hand is going to get you?"

They stared at each other for a moment. Then they both ran for the guest room. Rich caught up to Tommy on the stairs and practically ran over him to get there first. They opened the closet packed with old coats and clothes wrapped in plastic. Above the hanger rod was a wooden shelf holding a few dusty boxes. In the ceiling was the trapdoor.

Rich and Tommy got a chair. With help from his brother, Tommy climbed from the chair and got one foot on the shelf in the closet. Then he pulled himself up until he could push through the trapdoor and poke his head into the attic. It was a lot warmer up here and smelled like an old sweater. A little light came through a vent at one end, but it was mostly dark.

"Get out of the way," Rich said as he lunged through the trapdoor. For a moment they were both wedged there until Tommy wriggled free. Then he got out his penlight and shined it around. The bare rafters came together overhead and sloped down toward the front and rear walls of the house, like an upside-down V. The floor was made of planks laid across the rafters below, although they were hard to see through the clutter of boxes and junk.

"So what is it we're not supposed to see?" Tommy asked.

"I'm not sure yet," Rich said. "Shine that light over here—*not* in my face."

There were bundles of old magazines and newspapers, an antique sewing machine, boxes of glass jars, coffee cans full of rusty nails, mottled paint cans, a plug-in plastic Santa Claus, ancient suitcases, and a manual typewriter. The boys looked through it all but found nothing promising until they came across an old military footlocker that had their great-grandfather's name and "U.S. Army" stenciled on it.

"Cool!" Tommy said. "What do you think is in it?"

"How should I know?"

Rich went to open it but found it locked with a hasp and an old rusted padlock. He grabbed the lock and twisted. It came off in his hand.

"Whoa, look out Superman!" Tommy shouted.

"It was so old, it just fell apart," Rich said, shaking the rust off his hand. Then he pulled the hasp open and lifted the lid. Both brothers leaned forward to peer in. The beam of the penlight showed them . . . nothing.

"It's empty," Tommy said with disappointment.

Rich grabbed the penlight and probed every corner, but the only thing he found was a hole in one side a few inches across. "Looks like rats took whatever was inside."

Tommy heard a soft thump from the closet beneath the trapdoor and froze. He could tell from the look on Rich's face that he'd heard it too.

"Mom and Grandma?" Tommy whispered.

"They shouldn't be back this soon," Rich replied in similarly hushed tones. "But if they catch us up here . . ."

Rich and Tommy scrambled back through the trapdoor, got it closed, shut the closet door, and put the chair back. Then they investigated the mysterious thump. However, the house was now completely quiet, and the car was still gone from the driveway. They decided something must have fallen over and went outside to play in the woods.

....

The boys' mother and grandmother didn't get back until late that afternoon, with a car full of bargains. After unpacking and examining their purchases, they took the boys out to dinner and then to the movies. It was late by the time they got home, and after the long day they had all had, they soon went to bed.

Tommy was exhausted and didn't have the energy to zap his big brother with his penlight more than once or twice before falling asleep. But not long after dozing off he was awakened by a scuffling sound on the rug near his bed. A lifetime of hearing about the Crispy Hand electrified him with fear. He scrambled for his penlight and flashed it wildly across the floor.

And there it was! Just as Grandma had always described, the Crispy Hand was poised there on its fingertips like some hideous black spider. Its charred skin glistened under the light, and it retreated a little.

Then Tommy noticed something else taking shape behind it. He was reluctant to move the flashlight beam off the hand, but it turned out that he didn't need to. The figure materializing in the center of the room glowed with a light of its own, a pale and eerie illumination like moonlight. It was a man, tall and hairy and clothed in a bulky coat that hung poorly on his thin frame. Tommy recognized him from the story—it was the stranger who had died in the jail. With still-mounting terror, Tommy realized that the right sleeve of the coat hung empty.

The stranger looked right at Tommy . . . *and smiled.*

Too frightened to move, Tommy watched as the stranger crouched down to the Crispy Hand. His empty sleeve brushed against it, and a ghostly hand emerged and joined with the man's arm. The Crispy Hand crumbled in a small pile of ash. The stranger stood, flexing his newly rejoined hand, and—after once more smiling at Tommy—faded away to nothing.

It was a minute before Tommy could even move. He just lay there, frozen in fear, his penlight shining on the spot where the Crispy Hand had been. Finally, he snapped out of it. "Rich! Wake up! Did you see that?"

Getting no response, he shined the penlight in his brother's face. But this time he received no threats or warnings. Rich did not move to shield his face. His bulging eyes did not so much as blink as they stared lifelessly at the ceiling. His slack mouth hung open. And his neck was streaked with sooty finger marks.

Suddenly Tommy knew why the ghostly stranger had been smiling. The Crispy Hand had been unable to kill the constable all those years ago and complete the stranger's revenge. But tonight it was finally able to fulfill its mission of vengeance—by killing the constable's great-grandson instead.

Where the Buffalo Roam

I knew Marlon from school, but not very well. The other boys who went on the trip with us I didn't know at all. They were Marlon's cousins and their friends, a few our age, most of them older.

The trip was Marlon's father's idea. He owned several businesses, including a dealership that sold motorcycles and all-terrain vehicles. He and his brothers and some friends went by the dealership and borrowed a bunch of four-wheeled ATVs. Then they drove the bikes and us kids way out in the Great Plains, where we could ride and make all the noise we wanted and not disturb a soul.

As I said, I didn't even know Marlon that well, so I was surprised when he asked me to go along. We'd been in the same class for years, but I had never been over to his house, and vice versa. This year, we shared the same lunch period and spent most of the time out on the basketball court. Somehow we ended up on a three-on-three team together with Keith Forney, and we clicked. We beat everybody.

But that was about the only thing we had in common. For one thing, Marlon smoked. I don't understand why anyone smokes. He doesn't understand what the big deal is. His best friend last year was Julian Johnson, but he was smoking in one of the bathrooms and set a bunch of paper towels on fire in one of the sinks. Julian got expelled for that, and his family moved to another school district. I guess that's how I got to be Marlon's new best friend—there was a vacancy.

When he first asked me about going on the trip, I started to think up excuses to get out of it. I mean, Marlon could play basketball, but he was trouble. Hanging out with him for 20 minutes a day while a teacher was watching was one thing. Tagging along with him out in the wilderness where he thought he could get away with anything was another.

But then he started talking about the four-wheelers. I had never ridden one before. My parents were more likely to get me a machine gun or a full-grown alligator than an ATV, and I really wanted to ride one. The thought of riding free across the plains, racing under the wide open sky, was just too sweet. I had to say yes.

And, I thought, who knows? Maybe Marlon and I would end up being the best of friends.

···········

We started out Friday afternoon. My mom dropped me off at Marlon's house, which I was a little nervous about. Mom didn't really know anything about Marlon, since he had never been over to our house. She didn't know his reputation for talking back to and swearing at teachers, or about his smoking, or about his suspension for stealing money from the school store. That was no big deal. How would she find out? It wasn't as if there was going to be a sign in the front yard advertising it. But she also didn't know about the ATVs. I had told her we were all just going camping for the weekend. She never would have said yes if she had known I would be riding around on a four-wheeler.

She didn't know Marlon's parents, so it wouldn't be a problem—as long as she didn't see a bunch of ATVs sitting there when she dropped me off. I worried about this on the drive over and practiced in my mind being surprised so I could convince her I didn't know about them, but it turned out I had nothing to worry about. When we got there, all she saw was a half dozen men supervising a dozen or so boys in the loading of a couple of vans and pickup trucks.

I jumped out. Before I closed the door, Mom told me to have fun. That's exactly what I was planning on doing. I found Marlon playing keep-away with some of the others. They had swiped a baseball cap belonging to one of the younger boys and were tossing it around over his outstretched arms.

"Hey, Vic!" Marlon called. He threw the cap my way. I caught it and held it in front of me like I was baffled, giving the kid a chance to grab it out of my hands. I always did think that was a mean game.

"Sorry," I said as Marlon came over.

"No biggie," he said. "Throw your stuff in the red van. That's the one we're riding in. We'll be leaving in another ten minutes or so."

He introduced me to some of the other guys, his cousins and their friends. There were too many names and faces to remember. I just nodded and said "hey" and figured I'd sort them all out as we went along.

We got on the road soon after that and headed over to where Marlon's dad had his dealership. The ATVs were already loaded on trailers. We just had to hook them up to the trucks and vans, and then we were on our way again. Marlon's dad and one of his friends rode in the front of the van. I was in back with Marlon, two of his cousins, and their friends. One of them had a hand-held video game, so we decided to have a football tournament. Two people could play at once. We played in pairs, and then the winners played to determine the champion. I lost the first game to Marlon. He had a tendency to cheat, pulling the game out of my hands at key moments so I wouldn't tackle his receivers, but I didn't say anything. I was a guest, and I was going to get to ride an ATV all weekend for free, so I figured the least I could do was let him win one video game.

··········

It was dark by the time we got to where we were going. How Marlon's dad knew where we were was a mystery to me. After a couple of hours on the interstate, we drove an hour more on a two-lane road and then turned off onto a dirt track worn in the prairie grass. We seemed to follow that forever. Out my window, the plain seemed to roll away like a black sea. The only lights that didn't come from our vehicles were the moon and the stars. I had thought we were going to property he owned somewhere, but I overheard Marlon's dad say something to his friend about this being "government land."

"What if we get caught?" the other man asked.

Marlon's dad snorted. "Who's going to catch us? Nobody ever comes out here."

It shocked me that we were on land where we weren't supposed to be. I thought maybe I'd heard it wrong. Marlon's dad was an adult. He was supposed to do things by the rules. Then I realized that maybe Marlon was the troublemaker he was because that's the kind of person his father was. I wondered what I had gotten myself into.

••••••••••

Marlon's dad finally stopped the van at a spot that looked just like every other spot we had traveled past over the last 40 miles. I was just glad the trip was over. Everyone piled out, and confusion ruled the darkness for a while, until it was decided who was going to sleep where. I learned I was sharing a four-person tent with Marlon, one of his cousins, and another guy. I helped put up the tent and kept an eye on my backpack. I didn't want it to disappear in the confusion.

Marlon's dad dug a shallow pit and started a campfire with wood he had brought. After everyone had put up their tents and situated their sleeping bags, they gathered by the fire. A couple of coolers of drinks and sandwiches were opened, and we all dug in. I was starved and grabbed two sandwiches, not caring what kind they were. Then we all sat around the fire and ate and talked. A few of the guys wanted to take the ATVs out now, in the dark.

"Not on your lives," Marlon's father said. "I've got to sell those machines. I'm not going to have you out there wrecking them in the dark."

One of the men, Mr. Desmond, started telling stories— ghost stories, cowboy stories, all kinds of stories. Some of the others went off to watch the battery-powered television Marlon's father had brought or to horse around in the dark. Marlon himself went off with some of the others to sneak a smoke. But I stayed by the fire and listened to Mr. Desmond tell his stories. He told the tale of General Custer's defeat at

Little Bighorn and then another about a haunted riverboat on the Mississippi. He was talking about the Pony Express when two of the boys came running up.

"Look what we found in the grass!" one of them said, gesturing toward the other.

"What do you mean 'we'?" the second asked. "I found it." With both hands, he held out a stony object about eight inches long and pointed on one end.

"You've found yourself a flint spearhead," Mr. Desmond told them. "A nice one, too. You see, a couple of hundred years ago, the plains here were the domain of the buffalo, or the American bison. When the herds passed through here, they stretched as far as the eye can see. The Native American tribes survived by hunting the buffalo. They ate the meat, used the hides to keep warm, made needles from the bones, fashioned bowstrings from the sinews—they used every part of it. But the herds are gone these days, and most of the tribes with them. You've got yourselves a lucky find there, boys. A real piece of history."

I had to admit I was jealous. Maybe tomorrow, I decided, I'd do a little spearhead hunting myself—if I could spare some time from riding my ATV.

∙∙∙∙∙∙∙∙∙∙∙

We woke to the smell of bacon cooking and scrambled out of the tent. The adults had several camp stoves set up, as well as a long table filled with plates, forks, spoons, milk, cereal, scrambled eggs, donuts, orange juice, and other breakfast stuff. I got in line and filled a plate for myself, still hungry from the night before.

After breakfast, we started unloading the ATVs from the trailers and gassing them up. Soon the coarse growls of their motors shattered the quiet morning. Marlon knew I had never ridden one before and showed me the basics. Throttle, clutch, brake—it wasn't very hard. I practiced around the camp area while they finished gassing up the other bikes. By the time all of us boys were mounted up, I was feeling pretty comfortable driving my ATV.

One of Marlon's older cousins waved and then took off, heading away from camp. The rest of us followed, racing each other and jockeying for position. I looked behind me once, to see how close the others were, and noticed how the wide tires of our ATVs were mangling the turf, which was damp from recent rains. Behind us, the muddy ruts we left chased and crossed one another all the way back to camp. *At least we won't get lost,* I thought, feeling guilty about destroying that perfect stretch of grassy plain.

Though the land seemed flat, there were ridges and dips to zoom up and down, and before I knew it we were completely out of sight of the camp. The others went a little faster than I would have liked, but I didn't want to lose them, so I squeezed the throttle and kept up.

I started to space out after a while. The constant racket of the motors made it impossible to hear anything else. The wind rushed past as I shot along the sunny plains. This is what I had dreamed of, and it was exhilarating. But after a while it also got to be a little boring. I wondered how far we were going to ride. It was hard to tell what direction we were traveling in. We still seemed to be going straight away from camp. I wondered when we would start to head back. I had no idea how long a tank of gas would last, but we didn't have any spare gas, and there was no way to ask any of the others. I decided I would just have to trust the more experienced riders like Marlon to turn back when it was time. If not, we would have a long walk ahead of us.

I followed the others over a low hill without thinking about what might be on the other side. After so many miles of grassy plain, I just expected more of the same. And that's what I found. But there was something else as well.

As I passed over the top of the hill, lifted a bit out of my seat, I saw something other than the dull brown and green grass. An old Native American man was sitting on a colorful woven blanket. He was big, but his back was hunched over and he was wearing a robe of what I realized was probably buffalo skin. Two steely gray braids hung down to his lap. His face was etched with creases. He seemed like a statue carved from stone as he watched me head right for him. I managed to stop my ATV in the muck the others had churned up around him.

The other riders had stopped or were slowly coming back. One of the older cousins wheeled up right in front of the Native American. Everyone was throttling down, and I was right there, so I could hear their words.

"You should watch out," Marlon's cousin shouted. "You could get hurt."

"You are the ones who need to be more careful," the old man said, though there was no anger in his voice. In fact, a trace of a smile haunted his lips. "Your machines are scarring the earth and drowning out her music."

The boy laughed. "She'll get over it. Who owns this land anyway?"

The man shook his head solemnly. "No one owns the land, just as no one owns the air or the water or the sun."

"Yeah, right," the boy said. "Well, here. How about owning some mud?"

He gunned his throttle and spun his bike, kicking up mud at the old man as he tore away. The laughter of the others was drowned out by the growing roars of their engines. I was horrified that they would treat anyone this way, especially an old man! I was close enough that by nudging my ATV forward just a little I could get between him and most of them. Mud and turf pelted me and my ATV for several seconds. Then, as the chorus of motors started to fade, I shut off my own bike and turned to the old man.

"Are you okay?"

The old man smiled at me. I noticed that he was wearing a necklace made from two short, curved buffalo horns braided with a rawhide thong. "Better than you, it would seem."

I shook off some of the mud. "I'm sorry about them. They're a bunch of jerks."

"They have no respect for the land, only for their noisy machines," he replied.

I suddenly felt self-conscious about sitting on one of those "noisy machines" myself. I shrugged. "This is my first time on one. I didn't know it would tear up the ground like this."

"Do not worry," the old man said. "That this concerns you shows you know respect for the land. The earth mother knows the difference between those who respect her and those who do not."

"Well, thanks," I said, feeling a little less guilty. "Anyway, I'm sorry we disturbed you. It was an honor to meet you."

I walked my ATV away from him about 50 feet, not in

the direction Marlon and the others had gone but in the opposite direction. I had had my fill of riding with them. After I started my ATV again, I headed back the way we had come. I stayed in my tracks all the way back so I would not do any more damage to the earth.

············

When I got back to camp, only the adults were there, playing cards under an awning and watching baseball on TV. They barely noticed me. I helped myself to some soda and sandwiches and then wandered off to eat. I wished there was some way I could go home. I should have known going anywhere with Marlon was a bad idea.

The others came back about an hour after me, arriving in a thunderous chorus that sounded like the world was ending. They were mud-spattered and were laughing and pushing each other as they abandoned their ATVs to get something to eat. I stayed off by myself until it started to get dark, looking for spearheads and just wanting the weekend to be over. I thought Mr. Desmond might tell more stories, which would help pass the time, but the boys played loud music and set off fireworks, driving the adults inside to play cards. I watched for a little while, glad the ground was so wet. Those idiots wouldn't care if they started a grass fire. Finally I went to bed.

············

I was awakened early the next morning by the shaking of the ground and a heavy rumble in the air that I could feel on my skin. At first I thought everyone was back on the ATVs already, but this sound was different, and Marlon and the others were still asleep around me. I crawled out of the tent to see what was going on.

The sound came from the north. I had to pick my way through camp, which was now a mess of churned mud littered with empty soda cans, sandwich wrappers, and burned-out fireworks. I made my way around a van, and then I could see it: a living carpet sweeping toward us across the plain, stretching from east to west. I didn't know what I was seeing at first and thought it was one giant, world-covering mass. Then I made out the drumming hooves of the individuals in the front, and I knew I was looking at an enormous buffalo herd. It was impossibly big, but here I was looking at it. I ran back to the tent to warn the others.

I grabbed Marlon and tried to rouse him, but he groggily told me to go back to sleep. I tried shaking the other boys in the tent.

"Get up! There's a herd of buffalo coming!"

They laughed sleepily and told me to leave them alone. Meanwhile, the ground trembled under the impact of millions of hooves. I ran back outside and was going to try to wake the adults, but the herd was almost upon us. I could see the wild eyes and foam-flecked muzzles of the bulls in front, and I knew there was no more time. I ran for Marlon's dad's van and scrambled up, climbing over the bumper to the spare tire and then to the roof, and threw myself flat.

The herd hit the camp like a tidal wave. The tents vanished under a sea of shaggy, humped backs. The noise they made would have drowned out all the ATVs yesterday, and the thick animal scent of them filled the air. I hung onto the top of the van as it rocked under me.

29

After a while, when it seemed as if a million beasts had already rushed past me, I raised myself a little to look to the north to see if the end of the herd was in sight, but the brown sea still stretched to the horizon. I did see something else, however. A little way from the camp, there was a clear spot in the herd, where the buffalo had parted to go around something. Staring, I saw the old Native American from yesterday. He looked back at me for a moment, expressionless, and then he walked on. As he moved among the herd, they continued to part around him, the only object on the plain that commanded respect from the stampeding animals.

I was getting hungry, but the herd continued to pass as the sun rose high and then began to settle in the west. As it grew dark, the mighty animals still continued their irresistible journey to the south. I wouldn't have thought I could sleep under such conditions, but finally, long after the moonrise, I fell asleep.

···········

When I woke up the next morning, the herd was gone and all was calm. Scanning all horizons from my vantage point on top of the van, I saw no trace of the buffalo. I saw no sign of my fellow campers either. The trucks and vans were still there, but the tents, the campfire, and the coolers of food were all gone. The ground that had been littered with trash and churned into mud was as grassy and undisturbed as when we had arrived. I saw no sign of buffalo tracks.

Finally I jumped down from the top of the van where I had sought refuge for the last 24 hours. I moved to where my tent had been and combed my fingers through the grass.

Nothing was there, not the slightest bit of stuffing from a torn sleeping bag, not any sign of Marlon and the others.

I went to the other vehicles and checked inside. There was no one else, no other survivor. I was alone. I did find some food in the van and wolfed it down, starved after a full day without eating. Then I climbed back on top of the van to take a better look around. There must be something left, I thought—a scrap of cloth in the grass, maybe. I looked all around in every direction for some telltale glimpse of color in the green-brown grass, but there was none. All that was left were the vans and trucks and a single ATV parked a dozen yards from camp on the dirt track that had led us here. I frowned at the muddy red machine, recognizing it as the one I had been riding two days before. That's not where I had left it, and I did not understand how it could be standing over there by itself, intact, when all the others had disappeared. I climbed down from the van and went over to investigate.

It was my ATV all right, and the key was still in it. The gas tank read full. And hanging from the handlebars was a necklace of rawhide braided around two short, curved buffalo horns—the same necklace the old man had been wearing.

His words came back to me: "The earth mother knows the difference between those who respect her and those who do not."

I climbed on the ATV, slipped the necklace over my head, and started the bike. Then I headed back the way we had come, following the dirt track across the open majesty of the Great Plains.

Attack of the Munchies

Randy knew he would just die if he didn't get to see *Night of the Demon-Beasts Two.* He was at his friend Ed's house the first time he saw the preview on TV. The two were supposed to be doing homework, but they turned the TV down low so Ed's parents wouldn't hear while they watched *World War Wrestling.* Sergeant Splat had just taken out Padoo the Killer Panda with a folding chair. Randy was turning away to take a drink from his can of soda when he heard the familiar *Demon-Beast* theme music, and he froze. Ed started to say something, but Randy shushed him and pressed closer to the small screen so he wouldn't miss a word.

"The people of Millersburg think their streets are safe," a somber voice intoned as the screen showed a quiet street late at night, with nice homes and big trees and bikes parked casually on the lawns. "One year ago a few teenagers stopped an invasion of infernal creatures bent on killing every man, woman, and child in town, and now they think the terror is over." A monstrous shadow rose from behind one of the parked cars. "They could not be more wrong."

A guitar screamed, and then the theme music played frantically as a sequence of frightened people in a variety of scenes blurred by too quickly to make out clearly. With a final glimpse of the quiet street, now alive with moving shadows, the chilling voice said, *"Night of the Demon-Beasts Two: Dark Migration.* Starts Friday at a theater near you."

"Whoa!" Randy breathed.

"We have to see that," Ed said. "We *have* to."

Randy nodded, still staring at the television even though the preview had been replaced by a cola commercial. "The first *Night of the Demon-Beasts* is my all-time favorite movie," he murmured.

"Mine too," Ed replied. "But I never got to see it at the theater, because it was rated R and my mom and dad wouldn't take me. I had to wait until it came out on video."

Randy shook his head. "It's not the same on video. Movies like this you have to see in a big, dark theater."

Ed frowned at his friend. "You saw the first *Demon-Beasts* on the big screen? Really? How?"

"My Uncle Ray took me. He's really cool. He'll let me see whatever I want, and we just tell my mom and dad we went to see something else."

"Oh, yeah," Ed said. "I remember you talking about him. He lives in Chicago, doesn't he?"

"Right, but he comes to visit every few months, and he's coming this weekend. He'll take me to see *Demon-Beasts Two*, no problem."

Ed sat up. "Do you think your uncle would let me come?"

Randy shrugged. "Sure. Like I said, he's really cool."

"All right!"

They high-fived, and Randy said, "Demon-Beasts, here we come!"

· · · · · · · · · · ·

Randy managed to videotape the TV commercial later that evening, and by Friday morning he had watched it dozens of times. He was so hyped about going to see the movie that he didn't know how he was going to make it through the school day.

Then disaster struck. The phone rang while he was eating breakfast. Even though she didn't say much, his mom's expression told him it was bad news. He just didn't know how bad until she hung up.

"That was your Uncle Ray," she said. "The transmission's gone out in his car, so he's not able to come now."

Randy tried to fend off the disappointment. "Can't he get another car? Or maybe we can go pick him up and bring him here."

His mom looked at him as if he had sprouted antlers. "It's four hours each way. Look, Randy, I know you were all worked up to see that new Disney movie. I'll tell you what. Your father and I will take you instead. It'll be a fun family night. What do you say?"

Randy's disappointment turned to dread. The Disney movie was just a cover—he and Uncle Ray were really seeing *Night of the Demon-Beasts Two.* Randy didn't think he could bear to sit through some stupid Disney movie while the masterpiece of horror he really wanted to see was playing in the next theater. But he couldn't tell his mom that. All he could say was "Great, Mom. That sounds great."

....

On top of everything else, Randy was going to have to let down Ed. The whole way to school he dreaded seeing his friend, not wanting to deliver the bad news. But instead of avoiding him, Randy decided to just get it over with.

"Hey!" Ed said when he spotted his friend. "All set to see the return of the Demon-Beasts?" He started stalking around like a Demon-Beast on the prowl and then noticed his friend's lack of enthusiasm. "What's wrong?"

"We can't go," Randy told him. "My uncle's stupid car broke down and he's not coming, so now I have to go to some stupid Disney movie with my mom and dad instead."

"Really?" Ed turned to his locker distractedly.

This wasn't the reaction Randy had been expecting. Where were the outrage and moaning and other expressions of disappointment?

"Sorry," Randy said.

Ed closed his locker. He still didn't look at all upset. In fact, he looked pretty cheerful.

"Don't worry about it," he said. "I have an idea. After your lunch period, meet me by the custodians' room, okay?"

Randy was too surprised to do anything else but agree.

···········

Randy didn't wait for the end of his lunch period to meet Ed. He was too curious. As soon as he finished eating, he headed for the custodians' room.

The door to the concrete-floored room was open. From the hall, Randy could see the racks of mops and brooms, utility sinks, a tool bench under a display of hanging tools, and the lawn mowers and other equipment used to maintain the school grounds. He saw no sign of the custodians, who must have been at lunch.

Randy waited around for 10 minutes before Ed appeared. He was carrying his book bag and seemed excited.

"So, what's going on?" Randy asked.

"Quick, in here," Ed said, ushering his friend into the custodians' room.

Randy felt a thrill of fear and excitement, being in a place where no kids were allowed. Ed led him across the concrete floor and past the covered lawn mowers to a steel garage-type door. Past it was a regular door made of flat metal, with no window.

"Where are we going?" Randy whispered.

"To the movies," Ed answered with a mischievous and calculated grin.

He opened the door, and Randy found himself looking outside into the bright afternoon. Beyond a small asphalt parking lot and a dumpster were the field behind the school and the traffic on Locust Street.

"Ditch class?" Randy asked, horrified by how much trouble they could get in.

Ed nodded enthusiastically. "The Demon-Beasts are waiting."

"But . . . but it's still rated R. We'll never get in."

"No problem," Ed assured him. "I've been talking to Rodney Severs. He's the one who told me we could sneak out of school through the custodians' room at lunchtime. He told me how we can get into the movie."

Randy was shocked. Rodney Severs got into more trouble than anyone else in his class. But he also knew that Rodney got away with causing trouble 10 times as often as he got caught. If anyone would know the best way to ditch class and sneak into a movie, it was Rodney.

"So what do you say?" Ed asked.

"I don't know. I mean, we could get in a lot of trouble."

"So what? So your parents won't take you to see the Disney movie tonight? Who cares! What's it going to be— Disney or the Demon-Beasts?"

Put that way, it wasn't much of a choice. Still, Randy was worried that they would get caught and be punished.

"I don't have my jacket," he said.

Ed reached into his book bag and pulled out Randy's *Green Bay Packers* jacket. "Good thing I know your locker combination."

Randy was out of excuses, and he suddenly recalled his excitement while watching the commercial for *Night of the Demon-Beasts Two*. He *had* to see that movie.

"Let's go."

•••••••••••

After crossing the field behind the school, they had only a short walk into town to the Walnut Hill Theater, with its six wonderful screens. As they continued to walk, Ed explained the plan.

"All we have to do is buy tickets for some other movie, one that isn't rated R. Then we sneak from that theater to the one where *Night of the Demon-Beasts Two* is playing."

"That's Rodney's great plan?" Randy scoffed. "Just switch theaters?"

"Hey, it works," Ed replied defensively. "And Rodney said it's even easier to do during the daytime. There aren't as many ushers, and they don't pay as much attention as they do at night. He said you just have to watch out for the manager. He doesn't like kids much."

Randy knew exactly who Ed was talking about. As long as Randy had been going to the movies at Walnut Hill, the manager had always been there, hunched awkwardly in his buttoned sport coat as if his body were somehow unnaturally twisted. His combed-back hair was bone white, and his shaggy eyebrows were the same shade. *Give me an excuse,* those eyes said, *and you'll never know what hit you.*

"Yeah," Randy agreed. "We should watch out for him."

···········

By the time they reached the theater, Randy was torn between his rabid desire to see *Night of the Demon-Beasts Two* and his fear of getting caught by the theater manager. But Ed showed no signs of nervousness. He chatted on and on about how cool the movie was going to be. Randy couldn't wimp out in front of his friend, so he tried to ignore his fears and focus on having a good time.

The front ticket windows were closed, with a sign telling patrons to purchase their tickets inside at the concession stand. Ed and Randy entered and found the lobby as deserted as Randy had ever seen it. The video games showed exciting previews to no one, and long velvet ropes corralled nonexistent crowds. The only people were two teenaged girls behind the concession counter. Even the popcorn machine was quiet.

But the place was filled with the smell of the movies, and despite his nervousness Randy felt a familiar excitement just being there. He was so flustered he almost requested a ticket for *Night of the Demon-Beasts Two,* but Ed jumped in and corrected him in time, requesting tickets to the Disney movie for each of them.

"You guys better hurry," the girl told them. "The lights just went down."

The other girl tore their tickets and directed them down the corridor to the correct theater. Ed and Randy headed in that direction. The corridor held the entrances to three theaters. The second was showing the Disney movie. The third, Randy saw with a surge of excitement, was showing *Night of the Demon-Beasts Two.*

"We've got it made!" Randy whispered, heading for the third theater.

But Ed grabbed his arm and pulled him toward the closed doors to the second theater. "Not yet," he said. *"Demon-Beasts* doesn't start for another 15 minutes. We don't want to sneak in until the lights go down, so we don't get caught."

As they reached the second theater, the doors opened. The manager emerged, his eyes locking on them instantly, and Randy's blood froze in his veins. The three of them stood staring at one another for a second. Randy felt the weight of those eyes—*give me an excuse*—and wondered how much of their conversation the man had heard. Randy struggled to clear his throat, but it felt too narrow to allow him to swallow.

Finally the manager spoke. "You're late. Show's already started."

He shifted to the side so that the boys could enter, as he held the door open. Ed went first, and Randy followed. As he passed the manager, close enough to touch, he had a wild fear that the man would reach out and grab him. But then he was inside the dark theater. The door swung closed behind them, with the manager on the other side.

"That was close," Ed muttered.

He and Randy stood in the darkness as previews played on the screen. The theater was about half full, mostly with little kids and their moms. When their eyes had adjusted to the dimness, they found seats at the back of the theater so they could exit quickly when the time came.

They waited, with Ed sneaking quick looks at his watch every couple of minutes. Finally he whispered, "We really got lucky."

"Tell me about it," Randy said. "I thought the manager was going to grab us for sure."

"No, I mean we're lucky that this theater is right next to the one where *Demon-Beasts Two* is playing. Only the matinee show is playing there. They don't use that theater very much."

Now that he mentioned it, Randy knew exactly what his friend was talking about. In the many times he had come to movies here, the sign for that third theater had almost always been blank.

"As long as they're using it today," Randy said. "That's what counts."

When the time came to switch theaters, Randy's nervousness was starting to get the better of him again. He was also beginning to get into the Disney movie, but he was going to see it tonight with his parents, anyway. So when Ed tapped him on the arm and stood to leave, Randy followed.

They slipped out the theater doors and found the corridor vacant. Ed rushed toward the last theater, where the matinee of *Night of the Demon-Beasts Two* was playing, but Randy grabbed his arm and stopped him.

"Wait. What if the manager is in there, like he was in the other theater?"

Ed looked doubtful for a moment, as if he had not considered that possibility. Then he shrugged. "We'll say we had to go to the bathroom and accidentally walked back into the wrong theater."

Randy had to admit that that was a pretty good plan, and he followed his friend. They opened the door to the darkened theater and stepped inside.

The previews playing on the screen provided enough light for them to see that they were all alone in the theater except for one man, who ignored them as he ate popcorn.

Ed led Randy down the center aisle, almost all the way to the front, and then made his way to the middle of the third row. The seats were the old-fashioned kind that folded closed like the jaws of a crocodile when you tried to stand up.

"Sit down low," Ed said, demonstrating, "so if the manager looks in here, he won't see our heads."

Randy slid down in the seat next to Ed and finally allowed himself to relax a little. They were here in the theater. All they had to do was escape notice for the next couple of hours and they were in the clear—except for one thing. Randy groaned.

"What's wrong?" Ed asked.

"I have to go to the bathroom," Randy said. He hadn't gone all day. With all the stress of ditching school and sneaking into the theater, he hadn't noticed, but now that he had he knew he couldn't hold out for long.

"Well, you'd better go now and go fast if you don't want to miss the start of the movie," Ed advised.

Randy dreaded leaving the safe darkness of the theater for the revealing lights of the lobby, but he had no choice.

He stood and started to make his way past the vacant seats to the aisle.

"Wait a second," Ed whispered.

Randy looked back and found his friend holding out a folded five-dollar bill.

"As long as you're going to the lobby, get me a large popcorn and a soda. The smell of that guy's popcorn is giving me the munchies."

The thought of spending any more time in the lobby than he had to made Randy cringe. It would only increase his chances of running into the manager. But he didn't want to look like a chicken in front of Ed, so he took the bill and hurried from the theater.

The corridor outside was still vacant. He crossed the lobby to the restrooms and saw only the two girls behind the counter. He used the restroom and then returned to the concession counter to buy Ed's popcorn and soda. One girl filled his order while the other took his money, so the transaction took only half a minute. He headed back to the theater with the popcorn in one hand and the soda in the other. Still no sign of the manager. He turned as if to enter the second theater, just in case, but at the last minute darted to the third entrance. A half dozen pieces of popcorn tumbled to the floor as he maneuvered the door open. Then he was back in the comfortable darkness of the theater.

The movie had already started, but the opening credits were still playing so he hadn't missed much. The man with the popcorn was gone, he noticed, as he made his way down to the front. He hadn't seen anyone else in the lobby. The man must have left while Randy was in the restroom. Maybe the Demon-Beasts were too much for him!

As Randy moved down the aisle, he scanned the rows of empty seats for Ed's silhouette. But he reached the front of the theater without seeing his friend. He counted back three rows but still could see no sign of his friend. He slipped into the third row, spilling more popcorn, and made his way toward the center of the theater, where they had been sitting.

"Ed?" he whispered. He suddenly realized that his friend was probably playing a joke, and it made him angry. "This isn't funny. You're going to get us caught."

He thought that would make his friend emerge, but there was still no sign of Ed. Then he noticed something moving back by the main aisle where he had spilled the popcorn. A shadow flickered, and then the popcorn was gone. He jerked away in surprise, spilling more popcorn. It fell on the seats in front of him, but instead of it getting caught between the folded cushions, as he would have expected, the seats snapped it up like hungry young robins at feeding time. As they did, Randy caught a glimpse of black mouths filled with jagged teeth and flicking tongues.

He staggered away from them in fright, spilling popcorn everywhere. All around him the seats thrashed and chewed, and then long, warty tongues, like black tentacles, came forth in search of more.

Randy dropped the soda and the popcorn bucket and climbed over the first two rows of seats to the front of the theater. The seats chomped at him as he climbed over them, but he moved with a speed fueled by terror. He reached the front of the theater and pressed himself to the wall. Right above him, the movie played over the screen, and he had to shield his eyes against its brightness.

43

As he peered into the darkness, he could see that the theater was alive with tentacle-tongues probing, searching for more food. With a horror that made him cry out, he suddenly realized what must have happened to Ed and the man with the popcorn.

The tongues searched the theater floor but didn't come near him. He seemed to be safe for the moment. But they also blocked his only path of escape.

Then a light showed at the other end of the theater as the doors opened. A familiar, dreaded figure peered in, but Randy was desperate.

"Help!" he called to the manager.

Even from that distance, he could feel the disturbing weight of the man's gaze. For a moment, Randy was afraid he was going to leave and abandon him to his fate. But then the manager flicked on a flashlight and moved confidently down the center aisle. Where the flashlight beam touched, the tentacle-tongues retreated with the speed of snapped rubber bands.

He stopped about halfway down the aisle.

"Got you trapped, do they?" he asked. He shined the light down to the floor at the front of the theater, clearing the area right in front of Randy. "Just follow the light on the floor. They don't like the light. That's why they wouldn't get you up by the screen. It's too bright for them."

Randy did as the man said, moving safely to the foot of the aisle in the circle of light.

"What are they?" Randy asked quietly, as if afraid that speaking too loudly would provoke an attack.

The manager shrugged. "I'm not really sure," he said. "They just sort of showed up here a few years ago. Maybe some alien creature that mimics movie seats to catch falling candy and popcorn? Something that evolved here in the darkness of the theater?"

As Randy continued to follow the circle of light on the floor, the manager backed up the aisle toward the doors.

"They're dormant when the house lights are on," the manager said, "but once the lights go down and the movie begins, they awaken."

Just outside the circle of light, the tentacle-tongues twisted and thrashed, as if frustrated by the nearness of food they couldn't get to. The manager reached the doors when Randy was about halfway up the aisle.

"But, if you know about them," Randy said, "why don't you tell someone?"

The manager grinned, and his teeth reminded Randy of the glimpse he had had of the teeth in the seats.

"Why would I want to do that? These creatures, whatever they are, leave the theater neat and clean. Kids like you leave soda and popcorn and candy everywhere. These things are a theater manager's dream. As far as I'm concerned, they're right where they ought to be. You, on the other hand, sneaked into the wrong theater, my young friend."

He flicked off the flashlight. As he slipped out the theater doors, Randy heard him say "Enjoy the show."

On the screen, a girl hiding in a dark forest screamed as the Demon-Beasts closed in. Randy, feeling something wrap around his ankle in the darkness, added his voice to hers.

Rising Terror

Lightning flickered over the valley, silhouetting the dark mountains that loomed all around, making me feel as if I were at the bottom of some deep, dark pit. So much rain filled the air that moving around seemed like swimming. Despite my slicker, I was wet to the skin and constantly feeling the cold trickle of the rain. But I ignored it, as did the other scouts and volunteers struggling in the darkness to save our town from the rain-swollen river.

"Give me a hand here, Steve," Mr. Baxter said. A half dozen cars and trucks were parked facing the sand-bagged riverbank, but even with the help of their headlights I could barely see through the rain and darkness. I made my way to help him heft a filled sandbag. Together we hauled it to the dike, almost 4 feet high now, and heaved it on top. On the other side, the muddy river water churned with the fury of a caged animal. I had a horrible feeling that it would soon break free with a terrible revenge.

The ferocious rainstorm had gone on for almost two days now and showed no sign of stopping. Things hadn't gotten really bad until this morning. With school canceled, my friends and I were free to help with the sandbagging. After a whole day of shoveling sand into bags and throwing them onto the dike, my arms and back were numb with fatigue. My hands were so tired I could barely make a fist.

But this was our town, so we kept going. My house, the one where I had lived all my life with my mom and my sister, was only two blocks from the river. With the water as high as it was now, without the dike we would have been flooded for sure. Even worse, if the dam upriver were to give way, the wall of water rushing through the valley would be so mighty it would destroy our house completely. But there wasn't much I could do, so I filled sandbags, as long as they let me.

Our efforts had pretty much destroyed Riverside Park, turning it into a muddy wreck. Behind us, across River Road, which was our town's main street, the storefronts were all dark. The only light came from Bert's Riverside Café, which had been turned into our flood-fighting headquarters. Bert had been in there cooking and making coffee all day. It's where my friends and I had eaten and where we went to dry off and rest every couple of hours.

I was looking over at the cozy warm glow from Bert's, yearning for another cup of hot chocolate, when I saw a group of men running toward us from the café. I recognized Mayor Whiting by the white cowboy hat he was always wearing, and I got a bad feeling in my stomach. We had worked too long and too hard for it all to end now.

The men split up and went to different groups of sandbaggers along the river. I stopped shoveling sand so I could listen as Mayor Whiting ran up and talked to Mr. Baxter.

"Time to leave, Mike," he shouted over the rush of the rain and the river. "They've got the gates full open on the dam, and the river's just topped it. They don't know if it's going to hold. Everybody's got to get out of the valley *now*."

Mr. Baxter didn't seem surprised, just disappointed like the rest of us. After the mayor moved on, Mr. Baxter took off his hat and stared out at the river for a minute, mindless of the rain. His house was just down the street from mine, and his business, a lumberyard a little way up the valley, was threatened too. If the dam went, he would lose it all.

But after a moment he slapped his hat back on, took a deep breath, and called for our attention. "Listen up, boys. We've done all we can here. It's time to leave the valley and meet up with our families in Johnsville."

Nobody moved at first. We just stood there with our shovels and sandbags. We all knew what leaving meant. Within an hour, the river would catch up with our sandbagging efforts. First the water would start to trickle over the top, then it would flow steadily. Soon the wall of sandbags would weaken and collapse, allowing the water to wash through the streets of our town. All our hard work would have been for nothing.

But if the dam gave way, the water would sweep over the sandbags and wipe out our homes, whether we were here or not, and Mr. Baxter knew it.

"Move!" he commanded. "Bring your tools. Greg, Paul, Bob, Pat, Steve—you come with me. The rest of you go with Mr. Frederick. Hustle!"

Carrying my shovel, I joined the other boys following Mr. Baxter to where his big Jeep Grand Cherokee was parked. We tossed our tools in back and then climbed in the front seats. Water ran off our slickers, soaking the seats, but Mr. Baxter didn't seem to mind.

When we were all in, he said, "I'm going to go check and make sure Mr. Frederick and the others are all set. Sit tight. I'll be right back." He climbed out again and shut the door.

"It feels good to be out of the rain," Paul said, pulling off his hat. Under it, his red hair was drenched and matted.

Greg pulled off his glasses and tried to wipe them with his sleeve. "I feel like I'm never going to be dry again. My whole body is turning into a prune!"

"Oh no," Bob said, rifling through all of his pockets.

"What's the matter?" I asked wearily. He was always causing trouble of some sort, always trying to get attention.

"I lost my pocketknife," Bob said, giving up searching his pockets. "I was using it to cut twine to tie the sandbags closed. I must have left it on the box of twine."

He started groping for the door handle.

"What are you doing?" demanded Pat, who was sitting right next to him.

"Going back for my knife," Bob said. "I know exactly where it is."

Pat grabbed his arm. "Mr. Baxter said to wait here."

"We can't leave until he gets back, anyway," Bob argued. "It'll just take a minute."

He threw the door open and slid out, his slicker pulling away from Pat's grasp.

"Idiot," Pat muttered. "We ought to leave him."

I watched Bob's slicker, a yellow blur, disappear into the dark rain, too tired to comment. The rest of us sat there in exhausted silence.

After a few minutes, the driver's door opened. Mr. Baxter climbed in and glanced back at us. "Everyone ready?" he asked. But before we could answer, his face grew hard with concern. "Who's missing?"

"Bob," Pat said. "He went back to get his pocketknife. We tried to stop him. . . ."

"He should have been back by now," Paul said. "He left pretty much right after you did."

Mr. Baxter heaved an exasperated sigh and checked his watch. Then he opened his door again.

"No one," he said, "and I mean *no one*, is to leave this truck. Got it?"

We all agreed. He slammed the door pretty hard, and then he too disappeared in the direction of the river. Across River Road, the lights had gone out in Bert's Riverside Café. The headlights that had been illuminating the dike for us were threading their way out of the park and flowing up the street in the direction of the bridge that would take us across the river and out of the valley to safety.

After a few minutes, our headlights were the only ones left. We waited in silence, exhausted. The rain continued to drum on the roof of the Jeep so relentlessly that it seemed as if it was trying to penetrate the metal roof to get at us. I shivered a little and wished for dry clothes.

The constant throbbing of the rain lulled us so that when the side door suddenly opened we all jerked around to look. Bob clambered back up onto the seat and managed to spray cold rainwater everywhere. The door closed behind him, and a moment later Mr. Baxter climbed into the driver's seat.

"Now," he said, "are we all ready?"

In seconds the big Jeep was jouncing through the darkness between the trunks of huge oak trees.

"Did you get your stupid knife?" Pat asked Bob, jabbing him in the ribs with his elbow.

Bob elbowed him back. "No," he said. "It must have fallen off the box. Water was already coming over the sandbags and covering the ground a few inches deep. I had to feel around for it. If I'd had a couple more minutes, I could have found it." He glared at the back of Mr. Baxter's head.

The rest of us were grimly silent. *Water was already coming over the sandbags,* he had said. That was it, then. The town would be flooded in the next half hour. Probably sooner.

············

We had almost reached River Road and cleared the park when the Jeep lurched and got hung up. Its engine roared, and its tires spun helplessly in the mud. Suddenly the town's fate dwindled in importance as it struck me that we might still be stuck here when the dike broke. But Mr. Baxter backed up the Jeep a few feet and with a running start bulled through the last few yards of mud, over the curb, and onto River Road. The ride got smoother as we gained speed and splashed our way down the dark street.

I relaxed back in my seat, watching our darkened town go past my window—probably for the last time. The baseball field was already underwater. The parking lot at the school was a lake.

"Ooh, look at that," Bob said, peering out his window.

Everyone leaned and craned to see, but I was on the wrong side of the Jeep.

"What is it?" I asked.

"The cemetery," Mr. Baxter answered grimly. "Looks like there was a mudslide."

The cemetery, I knew, stretched up the slope of the valley wall. As my imagination started to conjure images of what it would look like after a mudslide, I was glad I had missed seeing it.

Shortly after that, we reached the bridge that stretched over the river and connected our town with the interstate several miles farther along the road. But we had to pass through a couple of feet of water to get to the foot of the bridge. As the Jeep's headlights speared down its length, we could see cars stopped on the far side. Men were standing there, frantically waving their arms. I thought one of them was waving a white cowboy hat, but I couldn't be sure.

"What's going on?" Bob asked.

"I don't know," Mr. Baxter said. "Wait here."

He started to get out of the Jeep, but he stopped as a horrible screeching sound pierced the noise of the rain. As we all watched in astonishment, the far end of the bridge swung away from the cars on the opposite shore. The shrieks of its tortured steel continued to penetrate the night like nails on a chalkboard. Then the bridge snapped free on our end, tumbled away in the raging black waters, and disappeared. We suddenly found ourselves staring across a hundred yards of open water where the bridge had once been.

Mr. Baxter resettled himself in the driver's seat. He took a deep breath and blew it out. "Well, boys," he said. "It looks like we're moving on to Plan B."

"What's Plan B?" Bob asked.

"I'll let you know when I figure it out."

He got on his cellular phone and contacted the mayor, talking in a low voice while the rest of us continued to stare in shock at where the bridge used to be. We all knew what the loss of the bridge meant. The river was already over the bridge in Stockton, and the next bridge after that was 30 miles away. We were trapped here.

"Okay," Mr. Baxter announced when he got off the cellular phone, "this is what we're going to do. Mr. Kregg, who as you may know is our town funeral director, was the only person in town who did not evacuate his home earlier this afternoon. Since his house is the highest up the valley wall of any house in town, his decision might not have been as ill-advised as it sounds. So we are going to go visit Mr. Kregg and take advantage of his hospitality."

"What hospitality?" Pat grumbled. "He's the meanest man in town."

"He may be a sour old hermit," Mr. Baxter said cheerfully as he turned the Jeep around, "but even he will have to show a little consideration under these circumstances!"

"Maybe if we pay him," Bob said. "My dad says he's so cheap that he charges people for fancy expensive coffins and then buries them in plain old pine boxes so he can keep most of the money for himself."

"That's enough of that," Mr. Baxter said. "You know better than to listen to rumors. And since Mr. Kregg is going to be our host, you shouldn't speak ill of the man."

···········

As we headed back, Mr. Baxter switched on the radio. Maybe he wanted to hear the latest on the dam, or maybe he thought music would calm us. Either way, we were all quiet, thinking about staying with Mr. Kregg. When we passed the cemetery again, this time I was on the right side of the Jeep for a good view. Most of the slope had been wiped clean by the mudslide. At the bottom was a dark mess of oozing mud, headstones, and exposed coffins. I couldn't see well in the darkness, but the coffins I saw seemed pale. If there were any with the glossy dark finish of maple or mahogany, I couldn't see them.

When we reached town, we took side streets that led us higher up the valley wall until we reached a point where we were on the same level as the roofs of our houses down closer to the river. Mr. Baxter slowed the Jeep as we approached the short drive to Mr. Kregg's old house, with its steep gabled windows and the rounded tower on one corner. Lights showed through the curtains on the first floor. Mr. Baxter pulled up as close to the house as he could get, and then we all piled out.

He led us at a run up the stairs to the front porch. After being out of the rain for a little while, it seemed worse to have to go back into it, even for a few seconds. But soon we would be indoors, and we would have a chance to dry off properly.

Mr. Baxter had to knock on the door four or five times before Mr. Kregg answered it. Tall and lanky, he didn't open the screen door, watching us as if we were insects he was afraid might try to get into his house. His graying hair was slicked back from his face, which was drawn into wrinkles around his eyes and mouth. He wore the same black suit and shiny black shoes he always wore, except that the jacket was missing, revealing suspenders over his bony shoulders.

Mr. Baxter greeted him and explained that we had been sandbagging and had become trapped in the valley when the bridge washed away. He finished by saying "The boys and I would be most obliged if you'd let us weather out the night here with you."

Mr. Kregg squinted at Mr. Baxter as if he did not understand. Then he shook his head. "No," he said, and started to close the door.

"Wait!" Mr. Baxter protested. "You don't understand. We have nowhere else to go. If the dam goes, this will be the safest place in the valley."

"According to the radio," Mr. Kregg explained impatiently, "the dam has already gone. The waters should be here in five or ten minutes. You should have thought of that before getting yourselves trapped."

Again he started to close the door. Mr. Baxter grabbed at the screen door.

"Look, you miserable old man, whether you want us here or not . . ."

Mr. Kregg produced a shotgun from behind the door and leveled it at Mr. Baxter. "I repeat, you are unwelcome here. Leave my property immediately, or I shall be forced to defend it."

Mr. Baxter looked at Mr. Kregg as if he were crazy—as clearly he was—but then backed away from the door, ushering us behind him.

"Back to the Jeep, boys," he said as he moved away.

After Mr. Kregg closed his front door, we all breathed easier. "Heartless old lunatic," Mr. Baxter was muttering under his breath. But once we all got back in the Jeep, his usual good humor returned.

As he backed the Jeep out of the driveway, Bob asked, "Where are we going now, Mr. Baxter?"

"Not far, Bob," he answered.

He pulled the Jeep back out onto the street and parked at the curb.

"There," he said. "We're off Mr. Kregg's property and we are still at the highest part of the valley."

"Do you think he was telling the truth?" Pat asked.

"About the dam going?"

"I don't know," Mr. Baxter answered, turning up the radio. "But we'll soon find out."

As it turned out, Mr. Kregg had been right. The weight of the rain-swollen river had been too much, and the dam had crumbled. All that water was now rushing through the valley, scouring it clean of trees, houses—everything.

We didn't have to wait long for it. Looking out across the dark roofs of the town, we saw it come crashing into view, a wall of churning dark water as high as a house and as wide as the valley. Whole trees bobbed in it like clothespins in a washing machine. The Jeep shook, and a terrible rumbling filled the air as the angry river slammed through town. In an instant, the houses below us disappeared under the roiling water. Telephone poles toppled, cars flipped and tumbled, and the roofs of houses peeled away.

After the initial wall of water had passed through, the river continued to rage. The water came up to the floor of the Jeep, but no higher. We felt the power of the water as it sluiced through the streets of our town and carried it away. No one spoke. We watched the dark water and the parade of debris it carried from upriver—mobile homes, billboards, a vending machine, furniture. Nearby I saw an oblong wooden box catch in the upper branches of a tree that used to be 20 feet off the ground but were now at water level.

"Is that what I think it is?" Greg asked, pointing.

Before anyone could answer, the box seemed to shift and turn over.

My mouth was dry as I whispered, "Did something just fall out of it?"

We all stared at the coffin, waiting for something to happen, but as seconds passed it seemed as if it might have been only our imaginations and the rain.

Then Bob screamed. A figure rose slowly from the water in a shuffling walk, as if it were just walking up the road and hadn't noticed all the water. It wore a dark suit, and its face was inhumanly sunken.

Before we could recover from the sight of this figure, another slowly rose from the water. This one wore a tattered dress, and its mouth hung open. The two figures trudged up the driveway toward Mr. Kregg's house.

Before they had taken three steps, another figure appeared, and another. By the time the first two had reached Mr. Kregg's front door, dozens of others had risen from the dark water to join them, all in formal clothing that was badly tattered and deteriorated.

"They're all dead people," Bob breathed.

"The people he cheated," I said. "Buried in plain old pine boxes."

It's a sure thing Mr. Kregg didn't open the door for them, if he saw them coming, but after six or seven of them had reached the porch we saw the front door smashed open. Then they started to flood inside.

"We should do something," Pat said. "Shouldn't we?"

Mr. Baxter shook his head slowly, staring at the house. "This he brought on himself."

Half the dead people had entered the house when we heard the blast of the shotgun. It was repeated once, but no more. After a half minute, the dead people who were still outside stopped and waited while the others came back out. Then they all walked back toward the water—and us.

"What are they carrying?" Bob asked, straining to see.

I whispered my answer: "Mr. Kregg."

Six of them had him, carrying him high like pallbearers. He thrashed and struggled but could not seem to break free. When they reached the water, they did not pause or falter. They just kept walking until the water covered them as it had the rest of our town.

We all watched the spot where Mr. Kregg had disappeared for long seconds and then minutes, longer than any human being could survive.

Finally, Mr. Baxter started the Jeep's engine and drove us up Mr. Kregg's driveway, completely out of the water. After turning off the engine, he said quietly, "I'll put this to a vote. We can either spend the night here in the Jeep, cold and wet and uncomfortable, or we can go inside the house, dry off, warm up, and find some bedding. Who votes to stay here?"

It was unanimous. Even Mr. Baxter raised his hand. We spent the night in the Jeep, but I don't believe any of us, despite our exhaustion, did much sleeping.

···········

The National Guard came in motorboats and rescued us the next morning. The rain had stopped and the water had already gone down quite a bit, but our homes were gone. The process of rebuilding took years. But working together, just as we had that night sandbagging the river, we made our town as good as it had been before. Everybody helped—everybody except Mr. Kregg. His was the only house that was not destroyed, but he was never seen or heard of again after that dark night when the river took our town.

The Baby-sitter

—⟩·◇·⟨—

Monica Van Johnson was a 200-dollar girl with a 20-dollar allowance. She had been receiving the same 20 dollars every Friday for as long as she could remember. That was fine when she was seven and all she bought was bubble gum and Barbie clothes, but now she was twelve and had to keep up with the latest fashions. Clothes were a lot more expensive for her than for Barbie.

She marched into her father's den one night after dinner and announced, "I want a raise."

Her father, Dr. Van Johnson, looked up from his paper, unamused. "Pardon me?" he said.

"I want a raise," Monica repeated. "I've been getting paid the same twenty dollars forever, and it's just not enough. It's expensive being a girl. Other people get raises all the time. I want a raise."

Her father folded the paper and pushed up his glasses. "Other people get raises because they work. They do a good job, and they get more money. Do you see the connection?"

"Yes," Monica said sulkily. From the way her father was acting, she knew she wasn't going to get her raise. The only thing she was going to get was a lecture.

"If I give you more money, what exactly am I rewarding? You don't do chores. The housekeeper does all the cleaning.

The cook does all the cooking. What are you going to do for me that you haven't already been doing?"

Monica could think of no answer to this question that would not get her in more trouble, so she remained silent.

"As a matter of fact," her father said. "What am I paying you for now?"

Again Monica could not answer.

"Nothing," he said. "Twenty dollars a week is a lot for nothing." He sat back in his chair and opened the newspaper again. "We'd better make that ten dollars a week."

Monica felt as if she'd been punched in the stomach. "What? You can't do that!"

He spared her a cool look. "I can. I have. It's done. Ten dollars a week."

"That's not fair," Monica protested. "You and Mom make tons of money!"

This was true. They lived in an enormous house, bought new cars every year, and took annual vacations to exotic places. Monica's parents were wealthier than any of her friends' parents, and yet her allowance was suddenly lower than any of theirs.

"Yes, we do make a lot of money," her father admitted. "And that's just it—it's *our* money. My brother, your Uncle Jim, was a blood-sucking lazybones like you, Monica. He wanted his parents to give him everything, and he wanted to do nothing. Well, the world doesn't work like that. If you want more money, you'll have to do what everyone else does—earn it."

....

Monica took her case to her mother, but Mrs. Van Johnson failed to see the tragic injustice that had occurred.

"Maybe your father's right," Mrs. Van Johnson said. She was sitting in front of her computer and typing.

"He's *not* right," Monica said quickly, and crossed her arms. "He's evil."

"Your father isn't evil," her mother said patiently. "He just doesn't want you to rely on us for everything."

"So what am I supposed to do? Quit school and get a job?"

"Of course not," her mother assured her. "You don't have to quit school."

"A job? Are you serious? I'm 12. What kind of job can I get?"

Her mother sighed and stopped typing, finally devoting all her attention to her daughter's problem. Monica felt smug satisfaction. Her mom was stumped. When she realized there wasn't any job Monica could do, she would have to give in and talk her father into raising her allowance.

"You could get a paper route," Mrs. Johnson suggested.

Monica was horrified. "Do you know how *early* you have to get up to do that? I'd be a zombie all day."

"Well, we couldn't have you joining the ranks of the undead. Hmm."

As her mother thought, Monica's hopes rose, only to crash once again.

"You could baby-sit."

"Baby-sit?" Monica was shocked.

"Sure," her mom said. "As a matter of fact, I know a few people right here in Sylvan Woods who have been having a hard time finding a sitter. And you would be close enough to walk or ride your bike."

Monica opened her mouth to shoot down her mother's idea but stopped herself. She didn't want to have to change diapers or clean up messes or listen to kids screaming, but she didn't think her mother would have much sympathy for these excuses.

"Just put up a notice at the clubhouse, and I'm sure you'll get all the business you can handle."

Her mom went back to typing, and Monica knew she was stuck. She could either try to live on 10 dollars a week—which wouldn't even buy her a decent pair of socks at the mall—or she could try baby-sitting.

••••••••••••

As it turned out, Monica didn't even have to bother posting her notice on the bulletin board. The woman behind the main desk at the Sylvan Woods clubhouse saw her and said, "Baby-sitting? Boy, did you come to the right place. I get two or three calls a day from residents looking for baby-sitters. Wait right there, I'll get you a list."

Before she knew it, Monica had to buy herself a notebook to keep track of her customers, her schedule, and, most important, the money she was making. She started out charging five dollars an hour, but she was in demand so much that her rates were soon more than twice that.

Some of the kids she baby-sat for were as nightmarish as she had imagined, crying or whining or making messes all the time. So she crossed them off her list. Enough people wanted her services that she could afford to be choosy. She only baby-sat for quiet, well-behaved kids, and for no more than two children at once. She spent most of her baby-sitting time doing homework or watching TV, and she got paid for it!

One of her best customers was the Hunter family. They were new to Sylvan Woods and very grateful to find someone to watch their four-year-old son, Eric. He was a cute kid, with dark hair like his parents and a solemn expression. The first time Monica baby-sat him, his parents said he could stay up as late as he wanted. But he was quiet and spent his time in front of the TV, leaving Monica free to do her homework and gab on the phone. His parents said he had already eaten, and, as they had predicted, he did not get hungry. However, the fridge was fully stocked, and Monica helped herself as they had invited her to.

"He's kind of a weird kid," she told her friend Debbie on the phone while she munched on an ice-cream bar, "but he's the easiest kid in the world to baby-sit. He just sits there."

"I can't believe how much you get paid for eating their food, talking on their phone, and watching their TV," Debbie said. "You are so lucky!"

Monica got even luckier when Eric's parents returned that first night. His father was a tall and energetic man, with dark hair and fair skin. He worked at home, trading stocks and bonds on his computer, and he had dreamy brown eyes that Monica could stare at all night. His wife was short and petite. Her skin seemed particularly pale against her lustrous black hair. They were attractive people and dressed nicely, Monica decided, though they could both use a little more time in the sun.

When they returned late that first evening, they were all smiles and practically glowing.

"How was the movie?" Monica asked them.

"Absolutely wonderful," Mrs. Hunter said. "It was so good to get out."

Monica wasn't sure what Mrs. Hunter did for a living, but she was pretty sure she worked at home like her husband.

"And dinner?" Monica asked. "What'd you have?"

"Mmm," Mr. Hunter said, smacking his lips. "Italian. And how was our Eric? He gave you no trouble, I trust?"

Monica gestured toward the couch, where Eric sat, slowly switching television channels with the remote control. "No trouble at all. He's been a little angel."

"Excellent," he said. "Monica, my wife and I are so grateful for your watching him. We wanted to get you something to demonstrate our appreciation."

Mrs. Hunter held out a fine gold bracelet. "Wow!" Monica exclaimed. "It's beautiful."

"Try it on," Mrs. Hunter said. She unclasped it and fastened it around Monica's outstretched wrist. "There."

Monica held her arm in front of her, admiring the way the gold glistened.

"You're sure you like it?" Mr. Hunter asked.

"Way sure," Monica said. She couldn't believe they had given her something this nice. Debbie would flip when she saw it. But she would have to keep it hidden from her parents. They might think it was too extravagant a gift and make her give it back.

"That's wonderful," Mr. Hunter said. "If you'll step into my den, we can take care of your fee and see when you're available to come back. Since my wife and I both work here in the house, we welcome any opportunity to spend an evening out together."

Monica got her notebook, and she and Mr. Hunter made plans for her to baby-sit Eric once more that week, twice the following week, and three or four times during each of the three weeks after that. These were Monica's kind of customers—an easy kid to sit for, a well-stocked fridge, good pay, and free jewelry. As often as they wanted her, she would be available.

....

Monica wondered if maybe Eric had been quiet only that first night and would turn into a little demon like some of the other kids she sat for, but as the weeks passed he continued to be the quiet, well-behaved little boy she had met that first night. He never went to bed before his parents came home, but he always watched television and was never any trouble. She never even had to feed him. Basically, she just had to show up and keep herself occupied for a few hours. For this she was well paid, and the Hunters continued to bring her small gifts when they returned home—a silk scarf, a bottle of perfume, a new personal CD player.

Their home started to feel like her home. With all of her baby-sitting jobs, she spent more time there than anywhere else. Monica was at the Hunters' even more than she was at her parents' house. She was completely comfortable using their computer to do her homework, fixing herself snacks in their kitchen, and watching TV upstairs in the guest room so that Eric could watch the TV downstairs.

Being somewhat nosy, she had peeked in all of the cupboards and poked around in all of the drawers by the end of her second night there. Most of the rooms were decorated with antiques, which seemed to be Mrs. Hunter's business. The only place Monica could not get into was the basement, which was always kept locked for some reason. She figured there were probably more antiques down there, locked up for security, since the house had no burglar alarm.

Although Monica was 90 percent sure she was right, it bothered her that she could not find out for sure. She searched the house for a spare key but had no luck. For weeks, as soon as the Hunters left, she checked the basement door to see if they had accidentally forgotten to lock it so that she might slip downstairs and satisfy her curiosity. But they never did.

She would have felt funny asking the Hunters what was in the basement. If they found out she was so nosy, they might not trust her anymore, and her best baby-sitting job would be gone. However, she felt safe asking Eric what was down there. He just looked at her and then back at the TV.

"Such a little chatterbox," she muttered.

She went outside and walked around the house, hoping to spot a window that would give her a glimpse of what lay hidden in the basement. She did discover a few small windows right at ground level, but heavy black drapes prevented her from seeing anything on the other side.

After that, aside from checking the doorknob every night after the Hunters had left, she gave up on the basement. Her life was too full to be devoting so much time and energy to the mystery of the basement. She had clothing catalogs to order from, friends to call, boys to talk about.

Then, one night, the boy she talked about the most changed everything.

· · · · · · · · · · ·

His name was Kyle Harper, and he was considered to be the best-looking boy in Monica's class. He had blond hair and played every sport, although everyone agreed he wasn't too "jocky." He did well in his classes, and everyone—even his teachers—liked him. His wardrobe left something to be desired, consisting mostly of jeans and T-shirts, but Monica could live with that. Her biggest fantasy was taking him to the mall and dressing him in all the latest styles.

Debbie knew about Monica's crush on Kyle—all of her friends knew—so when she called Monica one night at the Hunters' with news about Kyle, she took great delight in making Monica beg for it.

"I just got a call from Jennifer Mountz," she said casually.

"Yeah, so what?" Monica said. "I don't care about Jennifer Mountz. I care about Kyle Harper. Do you have something to tell me about him or not?"

"I do," Debbie said, "but if you're going to be rude . . ."

"I'm sorry, I'm sorry," Monica said. "Just please tell me!"

"I'm trying. Where was I? Oh, yes—Jennifer Mountz. You know, her brother Joe plays baseball with Kyle Harper."

"Yes . . . ," Monica said, trying to hurry her best friend along. This was excruciating.

"Well, they were in the locker room, talking, and Kyle said—are you ready for this?"

"Yes! What?"

"He said he likes you."

Monica stopped breathing. For a second it seemed as if the earth had ceased rotating.

"Kyle Harper likes *me?*" Monica said.

"Cross my heart and hope to die. That's what Jennifer said Joe said Kyle said, anyway."

Monica let herself fall backward on the bed in the Hunters' guest room.

"But that's not all," Debbie said. "Jennifer said Kyle is over at her house right now—they live in Sylvan Woods, too—and she told him that you lived there and were baby-sitting. And he asked where and said maybe he would drop by and see you, and she said she didn't know but she could call me and maybe I'd know, and . . ." She finally stopped for air and took a deep breath. "So should I tell them?"

Monica sat up on the bed. "Here? He wants to come here? Now? To see me?"

"Um, yeah. Haven't you been listening?"

"Of course you should tell them." She gave Debbie the Hunters' address and directions to the house. But then she started to have second thoughts. "Wait. Maybe this isn't such a great idea. I mean, I'm dressed for baby-sitting, not for seeing Kyle Harper."

"Too late," Debbie said. "Expect him soon."

And then she hung up.

"No!" Monica screamed. She rapidly dialed Debbie's number, but the line was busy. It really was too late. Kyle Harper was coming to see her.

Monica flew around the house, making sure everything was neat and in order, and then she locked herself in the bathroom and frantically brushed her hair, making sure she looked her best. She was so jumpy that when the doorbell rang she threw the brush across the bathroom.

She composed herself and answered the front door. There, as expected, stood Kyle Harper, looking a little lost, in a cute way, with his hands stuck in the back pockets of his jeans.

"Hi, Kyle, come on in."

He entered, looking around the foyer, with its fine Persian rug and tasteful antiques.

"Wow," he said. "This is quite a place."

Monica offered to show him around, taking him first upstairs and then through the downstairs. She ended at the door to the basement and explained that it was always locked and had been driving her crazy.

Kyle looked intrigued as he studied the door.

"See how the pins holding the hinges together are on this side of the door?" he said. "You can pop those out with a screwdriver and then slip the whole door out of the frame. That's how my dad gets my sister's room open when she locks herself out. If you can find a screwdriver, I can do it for you."

Monica knew there were bunches of tools in the garage and she was very tempted. But she imagined the Hunters coming home and finding her with their door off the hinges, and she resisted the temptation. This was her best baby-sitting job, and she wouldn't risk it just to find out what was in the basement. Or would she?

"No," she finally said. "That's okay. Are you hungry? There's all sorts of stuff in the fridge."

···········

Kyle stopped by the Hunters' to see Monica on other nights from time to time. But he wasn't there the night of the tornadoes. That night, Monica was at the Hunters' all by herself with Eric.

She found herself staring at the basement door. She had resisted using Kyle's hinge trick to open the door and satisfy her curiosity, mostly because she didn't want to lose a good thing. If the Hunters came home and found that she had broken into their basement, what could she say?

But tonight, as the TV beeped and flashed emergency messages warning of tornadoes in the area, she knew exactly what she could say: "I was worried about a tornado hitting the house and thought I should take Eric downstairs, just to be safe, but the basement door was locked."

They would believe that, wouldn't they? Monica went to the garage to get a screwdriver.

It took Monica about 10 minutes to pry the pins out of the hinges and wrestle the door from its frame. Then the dark cement stairs lay revealed before her. Outside, the storm winds howled.

"Sleepy," Eric suddenly said from right beside her, and she gave a small scream. She hadn't seen him move from the couch and wasn't used to his sneaking around. "Sleepy."

"You're sleepy?" Monica asked. This was a first. He had never gone to bed before his parents got home as long as she had been sitting for him. She had never even seen him yawn.

"Sleepy," he said.

"Okay, okay," Monica told him. "We'll take a quick look in the basement, and then I'll take you upstairs and tuck you in."

She reached out for his hand, and he took it in a firm little grip. Monica felt around on the wall inside the open doorway and found a light switch. The stairs went straight down and then turned sharply left at the bottom. The temperature seemed to drop 20 degrees as she descended the first step. She could see nothing of what lay in the basement yet and would not be able to until she reached the bottom of the steps.

"Sleepy!" Eric said again, his hand gripping Monica's tightly. Oddly, he didn't seem sleepy. If anything, he seemed more energetic than usual.

"Okay," Monica said as they climbed down the last few steps. "We'll go upstairs in a minute."

When they reached the bottom, all rational thoughts left her head when she saw what was there. The basement was almost empty and looked much like other basements she had been in, with a concrete floor and walls and with pipes and ducts running along the exposed rafters. The black drapes covering the windows were plain and undecorative.

But what stole Monica's breath and made her clutch the door frame to keep her balance were the three coffins, resting on sawhorses in the center of the basement. The first was full-sized, the second slightly smaller, and the third half the size of the first. All three were empty except for the teddy bear lying in the smallest.

"Sleepy!" Eric cried, pulling Monica into the basement and over to the smallest coffin. Maintaining his grip on Monica's hand, he snatched up the teddy bear with his free hand and hugged it to his chest.

"The teddy bear is Sleepy," Monica said as understanding dawned on her.

"It seems a more appropriate name for a dwarf," said a suave voice from behind her, "but try to explain that to a four-year-old."

Monica spun around to find Mr. and Mrs. Hunter standing casually at the bottom of the stairs. Their dark coats and dark hair shone with dampness from the rain.

"I—we—came down here because of the tornado warnings," Monica stammered.

"Yes," Mr. Hunter said. "The weather is quite frightful. That's why we're back early."

"Bad weather," Mrs. Hunter explained, "means bad hunting."

Monica noticed that she was trembling and gripped Eric's hand more tightly. With a sudden realization, she said, "You're vampires."

Mr. Hunter shrugged. "Guilty as charged."

"This is unfortunate," Mrs. Hunter said. "It has been so nice having you baby-sit for us."

Mr. Hunter nodded. "We do so enjoy hunting together, and your services have made that possible. Eric is still too young to join us. Until he's old enough, we really need a dependable baby-sitter so we can enjoy our evening outings together."

Terror made it hard for Monica to think. She kept imagining what it would feel like to have needlelike fangs sinking into the soft flesh of her throat. But as the Hunters' words started to sink in, she saw how she might talk herself out of that horrible fate—and make a little more money in the bargain.

"Nothing has to change," she said. "I promise not to tell anyone. I mean, who would believe me, anyway?"

Mrs. Hunter looked at her husband. "She has a point."

Monica breathed a sigh of relief. "Of course, I would have to charge you a little more—say, twenty dollars an hour—for the stress of keeping your secret."

Mr. and Mrs. Hunter shared a look, and then Mr. Hunter nodded. "And they call us bloodsuckers," he said, but he wore a smile. "Just kidding. That sounds more than reasonable. After all, victims are easy to find, but a good baby-sitter is a rare treasure."

As he returned his attention to Monica, he stopped speaking. His expression slowly changed to one of joy and wonder. Mrs. Hunter clapped her hands to her chest, glowing with parental pride.

Confused, Monica looked down at Eric. He still held her hand tightly, but she was shocked to find his little mouth clamped to her wrist, feeding greedily. Monica felt the warmth flowing from her and started to feel light-headed.

"Well, well," Mr. Hunter observed cheerfully. "Monica, it looks as if we won't be needing your services any longer after all."

Michele's Magical Make-Over

Everyone has something they don't like about themself. For Michele Jiffey, it was the fact that she was taller than everyone else in her school. She was taller than her older brothers and sisters, taller than her mom, and taller than all her teachers except for Mr. Dougal, the basketball coach.

She had been known as Jiffey the Giraffe since the third grade, and at the rate the rest of the slowpokes around her were growing she would be known as Jiffey the Giraffe long into high school. However, Michele was a practical girl. There was no way anyone could make her shorter—she had even checked with her doctor—so she just made the best of it. She played basketball instead of being a cheerleader like she wanted. She danced only with Craig Jones at the dances and slouched a little so they looked the same height. And she made friends with the other girls who were less than perfect and less than popular.

Besides being tall, Michele was observant. Nothing happened around her that she didn't notice. So when cheerleader Jodi Everly's face started to break out, Michele noticed—no matter how much makeup Jodi used. And when cheerleader Katie Farrell started to put on weight, Michele noticed—no matter how baggy the clothes she wore. And when Chantelle Moore, another cheerleader, began to smile and speak less and less, Michele was the first to notice that it was because her perfect teeth had started to bend and twist in all sorts of directions.

Everybody else noticed these things eventually, since they had a definite effect on the way the girls looked and acted. Even more, though, they noticed the changes that took place in Cory Mulgrew. Cory had long been one of Michele's friends, one of the other outcasts. She was fat, with an acne-ridden complexion and teeth that looked as if they didn't belong to her mouth.

At least, that was the way she used to look. When Jodi Everly's face broke out, Cory's cleared up. While Katie Farrell was gaining pound after pound, Cory was slimming down. And while Chantelle Moore's teeth were growing their separate ways, Cory's were lining up nice and straight in a perfect smile.

Everybody noticed the change in Cory—you would have to be blind and stupid not to—but only Michele noticed the coincidence of Cory's fantastic transformation happening at the same time as the sudden and tragic downfall of the three cheerleaders. There had to be a connection, Michele decided, and she was going to find out what it was.

Michele watched and waited for an opportunity. While Cory was having her student picture taken, one came. Cory left her book bag unguarded long enough for Michele to take a nice long look through it. Shoved into a notebook tucked all the way at the bottom, she found three photographs. The first was of Jodi Everly and had horrible blemishes drawn on her face in red pen. The second was of Katie Farrell, and her trim figure had been substantially bulked up with the help of a thick marker. The last photo was of Chantelle Moore. As Michele expected, her perfect smile had been changed with a black pen to a snaggly row of mismatched teeth. On the backs of the photos, odd and intricate symbols had been drawn, and they smelled slightly of spices.

Now Michele knew what was going on: Cory Mulgrew was a witch.

Michele tucked the photos away in her own book bag and sat back to think about what this discovery meant and how she could use it to get what *she* most wanted.

···········

Michele went over to Cory's house after school one day. Since they had played together for years, Cory's mom knew Michele and asked her in. Cory wasn't home from school yet—she had stayed to try out for one of the spots on the cheerleading squad that had opened when Katie, Jodi, and Chantelle dropped out. Cory's mom served cookies and lemonade and talked to Michele while they waited. She was so excited about the changes in Cory and her life. It was all she talked about.

"How did it happen?" Michele asked, though she knew very well how.

"A combination of diet and positive mental attitude," Mrs. Mulgrew said. "Over the summer, Cory went to visit my sister in Maine, and we started seeing changes soon after she came back. Can you believe it? My little girl, a cheerleader!"

From the way Mrs. Mulgrew went on, Michele decided she had no idea of how her daughter had really transformed herself and her life. Michele smiled with satisfaction. That was good. She could use that.

Cory came home a half hour later and seemed surprised to see Michele, but she was friendly enough. Michele suggested they go up to her room to talk.

"You're a witch, aren't you?" Michele exclaimed as soon as the door was closed.

"Wh-what?" Cory stammered.

"You're a witch. That's how you gave Katie your weight and Chantelle your teeth and Jodi your complexion."

Cory crossed her arms and went to sit on her bed. "That's ridiculous. There's no such thing as witches."

"You can't fool me," Michele said, smiling confidently. "You're a witch. I saw the pictures, the ones that you drew on of poor Katie and the others. As a matter of fact, I *have* the pictures!"

Cory started to look worried. She began to say something and stopped. Then she went for her book bag. She dumped it out on her bed and flipped through the pages of the notebook that had been on the bottom. No photographs fell out.

"What do you suppose would happen," Michele asked playfully, "if I tore up those pictures? Would Katie and Jodi and Chantelle go back to the way they were? And what about you? Would *you* go back to the way you were?"

"Yes," Cory snarled. "That's exactly what would happen."

"Whoa, wait, just calm down," Michele said, settling herself casually on the floor. "I didn't say I was going to do that. I just want you to trust me."

Cory laughed. "I guess I have to, don't I?"

"I guess so," Michele agreed. "So you're a witch, right?"

Cory shrugged. "Sort of, I suppose. My Aunt Phyllis in Maine, she's a witch. When I was visiting her this summer, she showed me how to do a few things."

"Like how to swap traits with other people."

Cory nodded.

"So you decided to use that little trick to do a little self-improvement."

Cory shrugged again. "Why should Katie and the others have all the fun? It's my turn to look perfect."

"I couldn't agree with you more," Michele said, "But you don't want to be selfish, do you? There are others who can use a little improving, too."

"Like you?" Cory suggested.

"You don't think I *like* being known as Jiffey the Giraffe, do you? All I want is for you to make me a few inches shorter so I don't stand out so much."

"I can't just make you shorter," Cory said. "I can only swap traits, remember? For you to get shorter, I have to make someone else taller."

"No problem," I said, having already figured this out on my own. "You can give my height to Paul Franklin. He wants to be taller so he can play basketball better."

"Okay. That'll work. But I'll need a picture of Paul so I can . . ."

Michele pulled a folded piece of newspaper from her pocket and handed it to her friend. Cory unfolded it and studied the photo of Paul in his basketball uniform that had appeared in the newspaper the previous week.

"Will that work?" Michele asked.

Cory nodded.

"Okay, and here's a picture of me. So, how long will it take to work?"

"Not long. It'll take me an hour or so to draw the designs on the back, but then it'll take effect right away."

"So I'll be shorter right away?"

"Uh-huh. Just like that." Cory snapped her fingers.

"But how am I going to explain that to people?"

"Don't worry about it," Cory told her. "Most people aren't that observant—most won't notice a thing. The rest will realize there's something different about you, but they won't know what it is. Besides, who's going to believe you actually got shorter? They'll just think you got your hair cut or something."

"Great!" Michele said. "I can't wait."

"So what about *my* pictures?" Cory said.

"Don't worry," Michele assured her. "They're safe in my room, and that's where they'll stay. You'll have my picture, so we'll be even. We're in this together now. We both have to keep the secret."

Cory thought about this and then agreed. "All right. It will be just our secret—the new and improved Cory and Michele."

....

The next morning when Michele got up, she measured herself against the door, and sure enough she was five inches shorter than she had been yesterday. Her mom commented that something seemed different about her, but she couldn't put her finger on it. At school, Michele caught people taking long, curious looks at her, but the only one who said anything was Mrs. Keel.

"Good morning, Michele. I like what you've done with your hair. Are you going to try out for the open slots on the cheerleading squad after school today?"

"You bet," Michele said, clapping her hands to her chest in excitement.

She stayed after school to try out, and she winked at Cory when she saw her there. By the end of the tryouts, both of them had been named to the cheerleading squad.

"Happy now?" Cory asked on their way out of school.

"Couldn't be happier," Michele assured her.

••••••••••

But that wasn't entirely true. Spending every day after school practicing with the other cheerleaders, made Michele more aware of some of her other flaws. Sure, she no longer towered over all the other girls, but they all had better features than she did. Melissa's perfect nose made Michele's look like a trumpet. Jackie's gorgeous blond hair made Michele's seem limp and lifeless. Carmen's flawless skin made Michele feel as if her own face were covered in sandpaper.

So Michele started to make a list, and she took pictures when no one was paying attention. One day after practice, she went to find Cory.

One of the cheerleaders' responsibilities was taking care of the school mascot. The students of Kensington Junior High were the Rams, but real rams could be mean and dangerous. So instead the school had a dwarf goat named Kenny.

He was black and white and stood about knee-high and was the cutest creature Michele had ever seen. During games and pep rallies, the cheerleaders put little ram horns on him and walked him around.

Michele found Cory feeding Kenny and changing his water in his room next to the gym. The little goat pranced around and played while Cory filled his food dish.

"Cory," Michele said, "we need to talk."

She told her friend what she had been thinking and then presented her with the photographs and a detailed list of which features to swap with which girl.

"You've got to be kidding!" Cory said.

"I'm not kidding. You didn't just settle for losing weight or clearing up your complexion. I want to be gorgeous, and you're going to make me gorgeous."

"Oh, I am, am I?" Cory said.

"That's right, and you're going to do it by the pep rally tomorrow so I can show off my beauty to the whole school."

"Are you out of your mind?" Cory demanded. "You've got half a dozen pictures here. I'll be up all night drawing the symbols on them."

"Thanks," Michele said, patting her on the back. "I knew you'd see it my way. After all—you don't want me tearing up those pictures I have in my room, do you?"

. . . .

The next morning, Michele jumped out of bed and headed straight toward the mirror, but nothing had changed overnight. So as soon as she got to school, she tracked down Cory.

"How come I'm not gorgeous yet?" Michele whispered as they walked down the hallway together.

"I didn't have time to finish the photos last night," Cory said. "I'll work on them during class if I get a chance."

"You'd better," Michele said. "I want to be gorgeous for the pep rally this afternoon."

Throughout the day, Michele took every opportunity to stop in a restroom and check herself in the mirror to see if Cory's changes had taken place yet. But toward the end of the day, when the cheerleaders were dismissed from class to get ready for the pep rally, she still had the same face she had woken up with.

"What's the deal?" Michele asked Cory as they met on the way to the gym.

"I'm almost done," Cory said. "Look, I'm supposed to get Kenny ready for the pep rally. If you come with me and help, I can put the finishing touches on your photos."

Michele agreed and went with Cory to the little room where Kenny the dwarf goat waited in his cage. While Michele let him out and started to brush him, Cory sat down in the corner and worked hard with her pen.

"Hey," Michele said to her friend. "I gave you six pictures to do, and none of the changes have taken effect. How can you finish them all at the same time?"

Cory looked up with a sinister grin on her face. "Because I'm not doing those pictures. I'm doing one of my own."

Before Michele could do more than frown, Cory had added the final stroke to the last symbol. A strange feeling passed over Michele. The world seemed to tremble, and she could feel herself changing. In front of her, poor Kenny looked terrified as he too started to change. He grew larger, and most of his hair disappeared. His snout flattened, and his face altered, shifting and growing until it was an exact duplicate of the face Michele had been studying in the mirror all day. Kenny the goat had turned into her!

She tried to speak, but her words came out as a strangled bleat. She looked down at herself, at her furry white and black legs and her hooves clicking on the tile floor.

Cory walked over, smiling cruelly. "Now that's a change for the better," she said.

Kenny, who now looked like Michele, yammered nonsense and started walking around on all fours.

"I figured it was a lot easier to cast this one spell instead of all those other spells you wanted," Cory explained. "Besides, I realized you're the type who's never happy. There's always going to be one more spell, someone with a better chin or prettier eyes. So now you don't have to worry about it anymore."

Some of the other cheerleaders came in, and Cory's expression changed to one of panic and concern. "Quick, get the school nurse!" she told the newcomers. "Michele fell and hit her head. She can't seem to talk or stand up!"

One of the girls ran to get the nurse while the others tried to calm down "Michele." Outside in the gym, the music for the pep rally started up. Cory scooped up Michele in her new goat form and hugged her to her chest. Together they watched the other cheerleaders try to calm down poor confused Kenny.

Cory laughed in Michele's ear. "And don't you worry about those pictures you hid in your room. I'll just have to visit my poor, crazy friend Michele at home until I find them."

Then she walked to the door and out into the gym. As the crowd filling the bleachers saw the goat in Cory's arms, a huge cheer went up.

"There you go," Cory said in Michele's ear. "You finally got what you wanted—everybody loves you!"

Hell on Wheels

On the first really warm day of spring, the sound of rushing water filled the air. The blazing sun had shrunk the snowbanks piled along the roadway from glacial mounds to occasional sparkling islands, and the gutters flowed with the runoff.

Pete was making his way home from school, mindful of the streams and puddles fed by the melting snow. Across the street from him, a bunch of other kids from his class walked together, talking and laughing and trying to splash each other with the water from the puddles. Pete pretended that he didn't notice them, as he did every day. Just as they didn't notice him.

He had lived here a year, ever since his dad had been transferred and his whole family had moved. His mom had found a new job right away and had made friends with Mrs. Grange next door. His little brother, Trey, was the most popular kid around, with three friends on their street alone. They had their own clubhouse in the backyard and called themselves the Davis Street Dragons. But Pete had trouble making friends. He had always had a hard time talking to new people, and here, in this town, they were all new people, even after a year.

Across the street, Eric Dorfmann had swiped Darlene Platt's hat and was running with it while she chased him.

She wasn't mad, though. She was laughing and calling Eric names. Darlene lived right next door to Pete but had spoken to him only once, right after he had moved in, when she had said hello to his mom and dad and his brother, too. She caught up with Eric and grabbed her hat back.

Pete watched his feet, stepping from dry spot to dry spot to avoid getting his shoes wet. He had just about reached the Billington gas station on the corner when he spotted something odd. A range of snow mountains had earlier surrounded the gas station parking lot, where the snow had been pushed into high mounds by snowplows. But the sun had been eating away at them all day. As the snow melted, debris from the parking lot lay exposed to the afternoon sun—a lot of gravel, a few colorful candy wrappers and soda cans, and a lost gas cap. But the thing that grabbed Pete's attention was a wheel, attached to something still buried in the icy mound.

He picked his way over to the wheel and grabbed it. It was about as wide as a silver dollar. He tugged, but whatever it was attached to was well anchored. Using his fingers like claws, he scooped away some of the snow covering it. He felt like an archaeologist in a movie as he cleared away the snow and the mysterious treasure beneath lay revealed.

It was a skateboard—black, with a flaming skull painted in orange and red in such a way that if you looked at it out of the corner of your eye the fire seemed to be real, rippling and burning. Maybe it was just the scrubbing it had received in the crisp, cold snow, but the skateboard looked brand new. Pete pried it out of the melting snowbank and shook off a few droplets of water. The hubs of the wheels were shiny steel in which he could see a warped reflection of himself. Not a speck of rust. He ran his hand across each of the wheels in turn. They all spun smoothly, with a whisper of bearings. It was in perfect condition, which made Pete think it could not have been buried in the snow very long. However, as deeply as it had been buried, it must have been plowed there during one of the big snows three or four weeks ago. He shrugged. It just must have been made out of really high-quality materials.

Pete suddenly thought to look around. Eric and Darlene and the rest were already two blocks away. No one at the gas station seemed to be paying any attention to him. There was a vacant lot next to the gas station and a self-storage facility across the street. No one was watching him. No one had seen him find the skateboard.

He was relieved, because he realized how much he wanted to keep it. There was no name or address on the board, and no houses were nearby where the owner might live. It must have fallen out of a car stopping for gas and then been plowed into the snowbank. The interstate was only a few blocks away and was the source of most of the gas station's business. Chances were that the owner of the skateboard had just been passing through the area. He or she was probably hundreds of miles away now and had most likely already forgotten about the skateboard. There was no reason in the world why Pete should not keep it.

He slipped the board under his arm and continued his walk home.

• • • • • • • • • • •

When he turned onto McCormick Street, Pete found the sidewalks clear and dry, though the gutters ran with melted snow and the echoes of cascading water rose from the storm drains. As he moved down the sidewalk, he felt an urge to try out his new skateboard. He had never owned one before. In fact, he had never even ridden one. His mom didn't think they were safe. But he had to try sometime if he was ever going to learn how to ride it. And he was still six or seven blocks from home. He knew he would probably fall down a lot while learning to ride it, and here no one he knew would see him. He stopped and put the skateboard down on the cement. The skull seemed to smile at him.

Pete knew he really shouldn't ride it without all the protective gear skateboarders wear—helmets, elbow pads, knee pads, gloves—but he told himself he wouldn't skate very long and would be extra careful. He put one foot on the board. Cautiously, he pushed himself forward with his other foot and then planted it on the board behind the first. He skimmed smoothly across the sidewalk.

This isn't too tough, he thought, pushing his back foot against the concrete a few times to build up speed. In fact, it was pretty easy!

Then he came to the end of the block. The sidewalk dipped down to the street, but a couple of inches of water flowed across it where it met the gutter. Without even thinking about it, Pete kicked hard off the sidewalk, building up speed, and sailed right through the water.

It was exhilarating! He pushed himself faster as he crossed the street and then shot through the water and back up onto the sidewalk. As he made his way down the next block, he tried shifting his body and his feet, and before he knew it he was zigzagging along the sidewalk with ease. When he reached the end of the block, he crouched low and cut a perfect turn around the corner onto his own street.

He couldn't believe it—he was a natural! His first time on a skateboard, and he was performing like a pro! The remaining blocks flew by until he reached his driveway. He shot up it, skidded sideways to a stop, and stomped deftly on the back of the board, which popped up obediently into his hands.

"Wow," he whispered, impressed by his own natural skill.

"Hey, you're pretty good," said a nearby voice. Pete almost fell down as he spun around. Darlene continued walking down her driveway but was smiling at him. "Is that a new board?"

Pete looked down at the board in his hands. After a few seconds, he recovered from his surprise and held it up where she could see it better. "Yeah. I just got it."

She removed the mail from her family's mailbox and walked back up the driveway, pausing to get a better look at the skateboard. She looked at the flaming skull and frowned.

"It's kind of creepy," she said. "I didn't even know you could skate."

Pete shrugged. "I didn't have a board."

Darlene laughed, the same laugh he was always hearing from across the street while he was walking home, but now she was looking at him and talking to him.

"I guess that would make it hard," she said. "You should bring it down to Borden Park sometime. Now that the weather is finally getting warmer, all kinds of kids will be there. A lot of them bring skateboards. I hang out with my friends there sometimes."

Pete nodded casually. "Maybe I'll see you there," he said. Darlene smiled. "Definitely."

....

The very next afternoon, Pete rode his new board to Borden Park. The sun ruled the sky again, unchallenged by any clouds, and the only snow left was a few dirty piles hidden in the shade. Pete wore only a light jacket, which fluttered and snapped behind him as he rode his new skateboard.

The park was full that afternoon, but if Darlene was there Pete didn't see her. He skated along the sidewalk around the perimeter of the park, watching boys and girls playing basketball, Frisbee™, hacky-sack, and other games. Other kids just watched or sat on benches or on the swings and talked. While skating by the playground, he saw a stretch of asphalt where a dozen or so skateboarders were hanging out, skating a slalom course around soda cans. As Pete skated up, the boy running the course took a turn too sharply. He went one way and his board went the other as the rest of the skateboarders laughed.

One boy, who seemed to be timing the contestants, dropped the wrist with his watch on it. He made a sound like a buzzer. "You're out, Glenn." Then he noticed Pete slowly skating past on his board. "Hey, Pete, right?" he called.

Pete nodded. Now he recognized the boy from his gym class—Zach.

"Want to give it a try?" he asked. "The time to beat is 37 seconds."

Pete shrugged. "Sure."

One of the boys directed him to the starting line, while another walked the course, explaining where Pete had to turn. It seemed pretty simple. Then he waited while Zach set his stopwatch.

"Go!" Zach yelled, and Pete launched himself forward. He crouched low for speed and zipped in and out of the first few cans.

"Wow!" he heard someone call.

He turned wide around another can and then started to build up speed again. When he hit the turn where Glenn had wiped out, he instinctively crouched down so low that he could grab the side of his board and hang on. After that, it was a breeze to reach the finish line.

"Twenty-nine seconds!" Zach announced as Pete skidded to a stop. "A new Borden Park record!"

After that, Pete was one of them. They spent the next couple of hours skating and practicing tricks until it got dark. Pete impressed them—and himself—with his seemingly natural ability to perform any trick they showed him.

"Man, you're pretty good," Zach said after Pete had managed to hit a bump, let his board spin 360 degrees under him, and then land on top of it again. "Are you going to the Skate-off this Saturday? You've got to go."

"What's that?" Pete asked.

"It's a big contest in the parking lot at Basinghill Mall, with a whole bunch of events. You can win all kinds of prizes, like new gear and gift certificates for skating stores."

Pete agreed that it sounded like fun and made plans with the rest of the skateboarders to go to the Skate-off on Saturday. Then they said good-bye and went their separate ways. As Pete skated toward home, he felt a little disappointed that he hadn't seen Darlene, but he was elated by the new friends he had made. And he looked forward to the Skate-off. Wouldn't it be great, he thought, if he actually won? What would he do with a gift certificate to a skating store, though? He already had a board. Of course, Darlene had thought it looked creepy, and he had to admit she was right. Maybe he would get a new one. . . .

The skateboard stopped dead on the sidewalk, while Pete continued forward. He slammed into the concrete and rolled, curling up as pain shot through his knee. He saw that he had scraped it on the sidewalk. His pants were torn, and his exposed knee was bloody. He glared back at the skateboard, which stood perfectly still. Then he stood, walked over to it, and picked it up. There was no crack or bump on the sidewalk. He used his hand to roll each of the wheels in turn. They all spun smoothly. As far as he could determine, there was no earthly reason why the board should have stopped so suddenly.

Disturbed, Pete walked the rest of the way home with the skateboard tucked under his arm.

· · · · · · · · · · ·

By Saturday, Pete had been back to the park several times and had regained his trust in the skateboard. But just in case he had also had his mom buy him a helmet and a set of pads. It wasn't too hard to convince her after she had seen his torn pants and scraped knee. But even though she disliked skateboards, she would not make him give it up— not after finding out that he had been going to the park and finally making friends.

The Skate-off was well attended, with dozens of contestants and hundreds of spectators. Pete performed well in the various events and particularly enjoyed jumping the ramps that had been set up and skating back and forth in the big fiberglass half-tube, shooting high in the air and doing flips and spins while hanging on to his board.

It was while he was waiting in line for his turn on the half-tube that he met Conner, an older boy with stringy blond hair tied back with a bandanna and a wealth of freckles on his tanned face. Conner was in front of Pete in line, and when he glanced back he looked at Pete's board oddly. Then he noticed Pete watching him and laughed.

"Sorry, man," he said. "I didn't mean to stare or anything. It's just that that board looks really familiar. Where'd you get it?"

Pete felt a spike of panic, afraid he was going to be accused of stealing it.

"My uncle gave it to me," he lied. "He bought it for me in California."

Conner nodded, not seeming suspicious at all. "That's wild. I used to know this kid, Kerry Drake, who had a board just like that. He was one great skater—as good as you."

"As good as . . . me?" Pete said, surprised to hear himself used as a yardstick to measure another skater's ability.

"Oh, yeah. I saw you skating earlier," Conner said. "Actually, the way you skate reminded me a lot of Kerry. You did a lot of the same tricks he used to do."

"Huh," Pete said, "so where's Kerry now?"

Conner's lips pressed together in an expression of sorrow. "He died, man. He was a world-class hotdog. Always showing off, always doing riskier and riskier stunts.

We were skating on an overpass they were building over the interstate. It wasn't finished yet. It just kind of stuck out over the interstate and ended, you know? Somehow—I still don't really know how it happened, and I was there—he ended up skating off the end and falling down into traffic. The reason I asked about the board, well . . . I know this sounds kind of dumb, but they never did find his board, and I just thought . . . "

He glanced at Pete's board and shook his head.

"No, now that I look, that couldn't be Kerry's board. The flames on yours look too real."

Pete skated when his turn came but then dropped out of the competition. When Zach and his other shocked friends asked why, Pete told them he wasn't feeling well.

Was this really Kerry Drake's board? he wondered. *Was Kerry's spirit somehow trapped inside it?* That sounded like nonsense, but it explained a few things. It explained how Pete, who had never skated before in his life, was suddenly good enough to beat everyone else around. And it explained what had happened the other day when the board had stopped, sending him flying. Had the skateboard sensed his thoughts about getting a new board and stopped as a warning?

Suddenly gripped by a very bad feeling, Pete carried his board home again that day instead of riding it, and when he got there he buried it deep in the back of his closet.

· · · · · · · · · · ·

By Monday he was rethinking his doubts. Other than the one instance when the board had suddenly stopped, he hadn't had any trouble with it. There must be a logical

93

explanation. Maybe a piece of gravel got in the bearings of one wheel, and it fell out when he went to check it. Sure. That made sense. That's what it must have been.

Besides, he missed the feeling of being on the board, of performing breathtaking stunts and hearing the oohs and ahs of the people watching. He was afraid his newfound friends would have no interest in him if he showed up at the park without a skateboard. Or, worse, what if one of them lent him a skateboard, a regular one, and he turned out to be a complete klutz? If the talent truly was in the skateboard and not in him, Pete would fall on his face time after time while everyone laughed at him.

Of course, he could just not go to the park anymore. But after a year of walking home alone and spending all his time by himself, Pete didn't want to give up his new friends. On the other hand, having no friends was better than what had happened to Kerry Drake, wasn't it?

These questions bothered Pete all through class on Monday. However, on the walk home, when Darlene and the others joined him, his mood lightened considerably—at least until Darlene asked, "So, where's your skateboard, Pete?"

"At home," he said. "I . . . forgot it."

"Not much you could do with it at school, anyway," Darlene said. "Are you going to the park today?"

"I'm not sure," Pete answered.

"Well, I am," Darlene said with a smile.

And suddenly Pete made up his mind.

....

When Pete arrived at the park, not only Darlene but also a whole group of other girls were watching the skaters, who were doing stunts and tricks to show off for their audience.

Pete had walked the whole way with the skateboard under his arm, but as soon as he saw the spectators he threw it down and hopped on. If anybody was going to impress Darlene, it was going to be him. He built up some speed and headed for a small plywood ramp that had been erected on the asphalt. The others heard him coming and turned to watch. Pete hit the ramp and then spun around in midair so that when he hit the asphalt again he was skating backward.

"All right, Pete!" Zach called after him.

Pete waved at Darlene, who smiled back.

Some of the other guys did jumps, but none of them was as good as Pete's. Then Zach did a new trick. He skated at a piece of plywood that was raised on a couple of soda cans. Just before he reached it, he jumped into the air. When his skateboard shot out the other side, he landed on it.

The girls watching applauded and whistled, and Zach took a bow. Even Darlene was clapping for him. It was more than Pete could bear.

"You think that's so great?" he shouted. "Watch this!"

He jumped on his board and kicked it up to full speed toward a park bench. Just before he reached it, he jumped all the way over and then landed on his skateboard on the far side. He glanced back to see how *that* had impressed Darlene, but instead of awe he saw concern on her face.

His hard landing had made the board go even faster. Facing forward again, he saw that he was shooting toward the busy street at an alarming speed. Not a big deal for a skater of his skill! He shifted his weight to turn, but nothing happened.

Now feeling the icy fingers of panic, he realized that the board was still speeding up. He tried harder to turn, but the board kept to a straight course. He tried to jump off, but it was as if his feet were glued to the board.

Then he shot over the curb behind a parked van. He tried to pry his feet from the board, with no success. And all the while, the skull on the board grinned up at him and the flames around it burned fiercely.

As he shot past the van and out into the street, the roar of a mighty engine drowned out his screams. Pete had a split-second glimpse of the bus's grille before it struck him. The impact knocked the skateboard tumbling through the air to land in the bed of a moving pickup truck half a block away.

············

When Doug's mom got home, she sent him out to the truck to bring in the groceries. That was when he found the skateboard. He had no idea how it got there, but it was his now. He had ridden his friend Kevin's board from time to time, but he wasn't as good as Kevin or any of their other friends because he didn't have his own board to practice on. But that was going to change.

He put the board down on the driveway and stepped on it. Now that he had his own board, he would show them! In no time, he would be doing stunts they wouldn't believe.